I0724942

AIR SERIES  BOOK 9

KRAMPUS

NOVELLA

AMANDA BOOLOODIAN

License Notes

Copyright © 2019 Amanda Booloodian
Cover Art by Deranged Doctor Design
Formatting by Michael Booloodian

Published by: Walton INK
Printed in the United States of America

ISBN-13: 978-1-947382-02-2

Walton INK
booloodian.com

License Notes

Copyright © 2019 Amanda Booloodian
Cover Art by Deranged Doctor Design
Formatting by Michael Booloodian

Published by: Walton INK
Printed in the United States of America

ISBN-13: 978-1-947382-03-9

Walton INK
booloodian.com

DEDICATION

I'm dedicating this to all the readers that were patient with me while trying to get this book published. Thank you!

CONTENTS

ONE

Tolman pointed his gun at Boone, ready to fire. Davis stepped out of a shadow. Without a thought, I waved a hand in her direction and she flew back. The whole world slowed.

I wanted to reach out to grab her and pull her back.

Trying to stop me, Vincent grabbed my arm with intense pressure, but it was too late. Davis struck the wall.

My eyes shot open with the impact.

A thud next to the bed made me reel back, unsure of where I was and what was happening.

Bed. My bed.

My room.

I was home.

As that realization hit, I remembered that I hadn't been alone when I fell asleep. That thought wasn't sinking in, not even when Vincent sat up on the floor next to the bed.

The dream. I had used my power against Davis in the dream. I couldn't have done the same to Vincent in my sleep.

Could I?

Neither of us moved. I could hear his breath coming in fast short bursts, just like my own.

"Vincent?"

"I fell asleep." His voice sounded almost monotone. A hint of fear slipped through.

"I must have woken you up. Did I... Are you okay?"

Vincent stood and strode across the room.

"Vincent?"

In the dim light of the room, I saw him grab his shoes. "This was a mistake."

"Wait. What was a mistake?" My heart felt like it was being squeezed. "Listen, I had a bad dream. I'm sorry—"

A burst of pain came from him. "Don't." The emotion was intense and filled the room, even though I wasn't reading the Path.

I realized he hadn't looked at me since we woke up. "You think we're a mistake?"

He stopped on his way to the door and half turned. "Tonight was a mistake." He balled up his fists, gripping his shoes. "I have to go."

Was I still in a nightmare?

I stared at the door, the bed still warm beside me.

What in the hell happened?

Before I thought too hard, I shoved myself out of bed. Pain in my wounded arm radiated through me, but I ignored it and dashed out of my room. I was at the top of the stairs when I heard Gran.

"Leavin' isn't the best idea," Gran said from the middle of the living room.

I made it halfway down the stairs when Vincent looked back at me, stopping me in my tracks.

"Staying might be a worse one," he said.

"You know I wouldn't be tellin' you this if it weren't true," Gran said

His face remained blank. "I can't take that risk."

As he left the house, I sank down on the stairs. He ignored Gran's advice. Gran, who was never wrong.

"That's one scared man," Gran said in a quiet voice.

"I'm not sure what I did." A part of me was convinced that I might still be asleep and the nightmare was continuing. Was it possible I was still in the jungle? Maybe I never really got away from the living nightmare we tracked.

"I don't think it's what you did, darlin'. Vincent would forgive you anything. The only one he doesn't forgive is himself."

The room was dark, so I sat on the stairs in silence for a while.

"Where's your sling?" Gran asked.

"I couldn't get comfortable sleeping with it."

"This wasn't exactly what you were expectin' your night to be, was it?"

I couldn't help but let out a small chuckle, even though it felt like I was falling. "Not even a little. He was so worried he'd hurt my arm that I could barely get him to put his arm around me."

"Well, you've been shot. Hard not to worry about it."

"I guess, but this hurts worse."

"He's just worked up. If you get all worked up with him, it'll make things worse."

"Is that what you saw?"

"Close enough."

I sniffed and shut my eyes tight when they burned with tears. "What should I do?"

"I wish I knew, sugar."

WHEN HE WAS GONE, my bed felt empty. He hadn't even shared it for a full night, and already it felt as if he belonged there. After a little tossing and turning, I gave up on sleep.

The air was chilled. It wasn't enough to make me miss the heat of the jungle, but I knew once the new year began, I'd be wishing to spend a day in that heavy heat. For now, I settled for a hot shower and warm clothes. It felt good to be back in jeans.

I heard voices in the kitchen, so I made my way downstairs. I expected to see Logan there, ready to start the day. Instead, it was Boone and Gran.

"Morning, sugar," Gran said. "I made breakfast for everyone, but you'll want to eat it fast. You're gonna have company this morning."

I wrinkled my nose up at the thought. "We just got home. It would be nice if we had a few days to breathe."

"I think Logan arranged for this one, or maybe Hank," Gran said. "You've got a little time. I'm sure Logan will fill you in. Eat up, though. You both look as though you've lost weight, and this doesn't feel like it's going to be a good day for anyone."

"Do you know who's coming?" I asked.

"I'm not sure. I'll be gone when they get here," Gran said.

"Where are you off to today?"

"Your mom needs my help with a few things," Gran said. "We're spending the day together."

Knowing how much caffeine I consumed in the jungle, I decided the coffee might not be a good idea. With unknown company coming, I was bound to be cranky regardless.

"I guess with people on the way, I should get ready," Boone said. "Thanks again for breakfast, Margaret."

To me, he already looked ready for the day, but I didn't say anything.

"What are you helping Mom with?" I asked before digging into breakfast.

Gran glanced out of the kitchen to the retreating Boone, and then took a seat beside me. Her shift in attitude rang alarm bells. "What's wrong?"

"Right before we lost you..." Gran started and trailed off.

"When I got trapped in the other world?" I asked, hoping she didn't know that I had died and been revived the last time I was away.

"Yes, right before you left, your stepdad found out he was sick."

"Sick? How sick?"

"The cancer's got him."

"That was months ago," I protested. "How come no one told me?"

"Bob didn't want anyone to know at first. At least not until he knew more. Then... well, your mom was worried about you when you didn't come home. Then you were in the city for a week and we knew you were having a hard time with Vincent being gone."

"But I was here." Tears sprang up in the corners of my eyes, but they didn't fall.

Gran patted my arm. "We didn't expect you to be gone as long as you were."

"Why isn't she telling me?"

"She knows you're home now, but she wanted to hold off on letting you know anything, but I think you need to know now."

A lump formed in my throat. "Why now? How bad is it?"

"This is going to be Bob's last Christmas."

"But there's chemo and radiation—"

Gran gripped my arm, cutting me off. "There's nothing they can do. It might prolong his life to try those treatments, but his quality of life wouldn't be good."

My cell phone started to ring. I ignored it while figuring out what to say. What could I say? I was driving by the time Mom remarried, so Bob and I never had a chance to get close. Nevertheless, he was my stepdad.

I sniffed and stared down at my plate, not really seeing it. "I should come with you today."

"Not today," Gran said, patting my arm again. "Bob wants everything to be business as usual. We're trying our best to make that happen. He's not telling anyone outside the family until after Christmas."

"Business as usual?"

"He's workin' today."

"Mom's not, though. That's definitely not business as usual."

"Your mom wants to get a better idea of what's coming. Today, I get to throw out the rest of her dead plants."

"Fake plants," I corrected automatically.

"Fake. Dead. Same thing. We're going out to dinner Friday night, though."

"I'll be there." It was an automatic response. The truth was, I didn't even know what day of the week it was. Or the date. How far away was Christmas? "How's Mom doing?"

"She's keepin' herself distracted mostly. You know how she is. Mostly, I think she's tryin' to distance herself from the situation until she's forced to deal with it."

"That sounds like her." My phone started ringing again. I glared at where it sat on the counter, but ignored it.

"Today is the first day she's wanted to look ahead to prepare herself."

"You mean psychically? She wants her power back?" Mom

suppressed her psychic tendencies as much as Gran embraced her own. "I've never seen her try to use her skills."

"She hasn't since your dad's been gone. She turned her back on everything that wasn't ordinary or predictable when he died. It'll take a long time for her to get back up to form, but she'll get there. She's very talented when she lets herself be."

Mom was losing her second husband. My dad had passed away when I was so young that I didn't even remember him. Knowing that she was losing Bob must be bringing up bad memories.

"Is there anything I can do?" I asked.

"Just act normal. Your mom needs that now."

I nodded; I knew I was going to cry if I said anything.

There was a knock on the back door, and Logan walked in. His new housemate, Renick, trailed behind, looking uncomfortable.

"Howdy," Logan said, grinning from ear to ear.

Gran smiled back, but for once, I didn't catch Logan's contagious smile.

"Mornin'," Gran said. "I've got breakfast ready, so eat up. You all have a big day ahead of you."

"Any hint on how it's going to go?" Logan asked.

"It's gonna go from bad to worse," Gran warned, "but it's tomorrow that you need to worry about."

"What happens tomorrow?" Logan asked.

"No idea, but it isn't gonna be fun for anyone," Gran said.

"At least we don't have to worry about that until tomorrow," Logan said.

"My ride is gonna be here soon." Gran patted my shoulder on the way by. "You all take care of yourselves today."

"Thank you, Margaret," Logan said as she disappeared into the living room.

Renick settled down to the business of breakfast, but as

soon as Gran was gone, Logan turned his focus to me. "What in tarnation happened this morning?"

"What do you mean?"

"Vincent called me to check on you. He thought something was wrong."

"What? Why?"

"He said you weren't picking up your phone."

I rolled my eyes. "I was busy."

"Better give him a call. He's got a burr under his saddle."

"Sure," I said, making no move to my phone. "I'll text him or something."

Logan shrugged and let the subject drop.

"Gran said we're having company," I said, steering the conversation away from Vincent.

"We do. Hank is bringing Kyrian here."

"Why?"

"Well, she thinks she's coming here to say a few nice words to your grandmother about you being missing," Logan said.

"She's not going to like what she finds when she gets here," Boone said, joining us.

"I thought we'd go into the office," I said. "It would be like pulling off a Band-Aid. Everyone would see we're alive all at once.

"Hank thought this way might be better," Logan said. "It'll give Kyrian some time with the information before everyone else knows."

"What are we telling her?" I asked.

"We'll want to stick close to the truth," Boone said.

"Agreed," Logan said. "Up to a point anyway. Renick and I talked about it last night. He'd rather stay out of it."

"As far as AIR or the military are concerned, I'd rather they think I died with the others," Renick said. "I don't want to live the rest of my life as a lab rat."

"It's up to you, of course," Boone said, "but what are you going to do?"

"The princess here has me set up," Renick said.

"What? I don't have anything," I said.

"Fenrir showed up with some friends of yours," Renick said. "Two batty old guys. They made me an offer."

My eyes narrowed. "They aren't friends."

"What kind of offer?" Boone asked.

Renick shrugged. "They're looking for people more in touch with what's going on in the world. I'll be working for them. It'll take them a while to set me up with a new ID. So until then, I'm cooling my heels."

"But what will you actually be doing?" Boone asked.

Renick shrugged and went back his bacon. "Just leave me out of it."

Boone looked like he wanted to ask more, but Logan interrupted.

"I think we can tell Kyrian everything up to the point where the others died. We killed them in self-defense, after all."

Was it really self-defense though? I thought about yanking on Davis's Path to get her out of the way. If I hadn't pulled so hard, maybe she'd still be alive.

Although, if she had survived, she would have killed me. I knew that.

At least some part of me did.

Logan's phone announced an incoming message. He frowned at the screen before typing a reply. "Vincent again."

"Is he on his way over?" Boone looked as though he was studiously avoiding looking in my direction. "It could work for us. Who's going to argue with a Walker?"

I wondered briefly how much he heard last night, but it probably didn't matter.

"True enough," Logan said. "He doesn't know the story, but Kyrian isn't likely to ask him much."

"Does he even talk to anyone at the office?" Renick asked.

"Not much," Logan admitted.

"That makes sense," Renick said. "No one wants to spend time with a Walker."

I wanted to kick Renick out, but I didn't think Boone would approve, and I knew Gran wouldn't.

It sounded sad to think of Vincent being that isolated. It was almost enough to make me grab the phone and call him, but I knew why he was calling. He must have sensed that I had gotten upset about Bob. He'd want to talk about it.

I, on the other hand, had no intention of dwelling on it at the moment.

"What about the rest?" I asked. "The military tried to kill us."

"I think playing ignorant might be our best bet there," Logan said. "We can say there were some explosions at camp while we were away. Our communications were gone, so we made our way home on our own."

It sounded like a sparse explanation and not a very believable one. "The whole way home without calling?"

"We can imply that we thought it was the military that attacked us," Boone said. "That might do the trick."

"We don't want any further retaliation on their part," Logan said.

"I don't think we'll have much," Boone said. "They'll deny it, we'll pretend to accept that, and hopefully everyone will move on."

"Is that what we want?" I asked. "I mean, they did try to kill us. Don't we want to know what happened?"

"Not openly," Boone said, "but we will want to find out who might want us dead. If there's a faction inside AIR and the military that are anti-Lost, it needs to be investigated carefully."

I thought that over. It made sense. If we made a big deal over it, they'd probably try to cover it up. Take us out of the picture.

"To investigate further, we might need more people on our side," I said. "I can't see how there's much we can do on our own."

"She has a point," Renick said. "If you find something, what are you going to do with the information? It sounds like you need someone higher up."

Logan sighed. "We'd need Kyrian for that, unless anyone has some pull higher up that we can rely on?"

"If we tell Kyrian everything, will she take our side?" Boone asked.

"Hard to say," Logan said.

"Actually, I think she'll back us up," I said. "Kyrian is ambitious. There have to be some people high up in the government involved. It could make some empty spaces for her to get a foot in the door."

"There's something to that," Logan said. "Do you all want to risk telling her everything?"

"What's the worst that can happen?" I asked.

"We all end up in jail or on the run," Boone answered immediately.

"It wouldn't be the first time I've been threatened with the prospect of jail," I said. "Kyrian backed me when the DC thought I killed Vincent."

"When did that happen?" Boone asked, looking surprised.

"Last time you were here, Vincent dealt with the changeling. He didn't come back for another week. That's a lot of time for an agent to be missing," I said.

"But he's a Walker," Boone said. "That's just dumb."

Renick snorted. "They probably thought anyone would want to snuff out a Walker."

"Kyrian kept me out of their hands until Vincent showed up," I said, glaring at Renick.

"You should have called me," Boone said. "I could have helped."

I shrugged. "Everyone that mattered knew I was innocent. It was only a matter of time before Vincent showed up."

"I guess we chance telling her," Logan said. "We might want to start thinking of a contingency plan in case things don't go the way we want them."

"What kind of contingency plan?" I asked.

"Princess, if the government wants you dead, you don't just let them kill you," Renick said. "You fight or you run."

"If Kyrian goes along with our plan of reporting the altered incident, I think we'll be in the clear," Boone said. "I say we give it a shot and tell her the truth."

"And me?" Renick said, looking hard at Boone.

"That one is up to you," Boone said.

"I'm dead," Renick said. "I think I need to stay that way."

Kyrian wasn't happy. She was surprised enough when I met her at the door to introduce her to Molly, but then the others filed into the living room—minus Renick, who had made himself scarce—and she was instantly suspicious.

Logan sat on the couch beside me. Boone stood behind us and the two of them explained everything we agreed on, from start to finish.

"So, you think someone in the military may still want you dead?" Kyrian asked.

"Possibly a faction inside AIR as well," Logan said. "There's something going on here that runs deeper than one case."

"Why trust me with this?" Kyrian asked, sounding skeptical.

I looked towards Logan, but he appeared to be waiting for me to respond. "You didn't let the military arrest me the last time they tried."

"You must know that that's an altogether different circumstance," Kyrian said.

My face began to color, and I tried to form the right words to explain her ambition is why we had chosen to talk with her. "If AIR is involved, then there are some very senior officials involved. If this comes to light, space could open up where someone with knowledge and experience with the Lost might aspire for."

Kyrian wore a tight-lipped smile. "Our first priority will be to get your story down. Hank will work with you on that. I want you all in the office this afternoon. Agent Heidrich, I want Dr. Yelton to look you over and document everything. That will help corroborate your story. Hank, keep this off the system until I've approved. It's very important that you all keep any suspicion of AIR and the military out of reports and don't share this information with anyone, even fellow agents."

"What about Agent Boone?" I asked, trying to mask the concern in my voice. "He's not assigned to this office."

Kyrian hesitated. "Hank can start the transfer paperwork to keep you here, but there are going to be people that want answers from him."

"I'll have to go back to the base," Boone said.

"No!" I said before I could stop myself. "If you're alone, you might not come back out of there."

"We can stall for a while," Kyrian said.

"I'll take what I can get," Boone said.

An intense uneasiness settled over me.

Kyrian shifted on the couch and turned her attention back to Logan. "Hank will take all of you into the office, including Agent Pironis and Agent Wolfe. You mentioned he was stabbed. He should visit Dr. Yelton as well."

"There's no wound left for Dr. Yelton to see," Logan said.

"Regardless," Kyrian said. "I want it documented. Boone, I want you up there as well. A concussion during the case might buy us some extra time."

Boone nodded and Kyrian looked us over for another long minute, but her mind seemed like it was elsewhere.

"What time do you want us in?" Logan asked.

"After two," Kyrian said. "Hank will have a more exact time. If you walk in with no one else knowing you're alive, it will cause a commotion. We can start floating the fact that you're alive and back. It'll spread fast around the office."

"That should be enough to cause less of a shock when you arrive," Hank said.

"Before anyone goes to see Dr. Yelton, I want you in the control room," Kyrian said. "I want people to be able to see for themselves that you're back. Your project was confidential—the other agents will accept it when you can't tell them anything. Hank will work up your reports. Is there anything else I should know?"

I looked towards Logan, hoping he would take the lead.

"We've said everything that you need to know," Logan said.

"Good. Keep the details sparse." Kyrian stood to leave. "Hank knows what to leave out of the reports. If anyone asks, I wasn't here today and I know nothing beyond what's written down."

Hours later, we discovered that Kyrian wasn't wrong about needing to spread the word before we arrived. The moment we walked into the control room, voices died away and everyone stared. It was as though we were frozen in two groups, the room of agents staring at us, and us staring back at them. I'd never been comfortable with people staring at me, but at least I wasn't alone this time.

Logan was the one who broke the silence.

"Howdy, all," he said, walking through the middle of the room and over to Hank.

"Let's grab a desk," I said under my breath while Logan held the room's attention.

The room started back up again as though rebooted. Agents stopped Logan to shake his hand.

I went the closest desk and dropped my bag. Agent Paulson came over before I had the chance to take a seat.

"We held out hopes of seeing you all again," Paulson said. "It's good to see you safe," he took in the sling I wore, "even if not completely sound."

"It's good to be back in the office," I said.

The room quieted again, and I looked up to see Rider and Vincent come in. Rider noticed us and came over, Vincent trailing behind.

"The gang's all here. Agent Boone, it's good to see you again," Paulson said. "Listen, a few of us got together, and we wanted to take you all out for drinks later this week. All of you," he added, making sure Boone knew he was included, "to celebrate your return."

"That sounds nice," I said, though I felt a little off balance. I'd never been invited out for drinks with coworkers. Looking around the room, I saw eyes drawn toward us again and again.

"Thanks," Boone said.

"Vincent, Rider, are you two up for it?" Paulson asked.

"I would like that," Rider said.

Vincent nodded. He looked uncomfortable with the preferential treatment from a coworker. It didn't surprise me, though. Before Vincent left, Paulson had been making a concentrated effort to treat Vincent as he would anyone else. I hoped that others in the office would take his lead. Going for drinks was a good start.

"Great," Paulson said. "I'll text you the time and place."

"I don't think any of us have phones anymore," I said, glancing at the others or confirmation.

"None of you?" Paulson asked. "No wonder everyone lost track of you. I'll talk to Hank to get your new numbers. I'm sure he'll have you geared up before you leave today."

"Sounds good," I said. "We need to make our way upstairs to Dr. Yelton."

"How bad is the arm?" Paulson asked.

I looked down at my arm in its sling. "Not as bad as it was, but we'll have to see what the doctor thinks."

"We'll catch up later, then." Paulson clapped Rider's shoulder before going back to work.

"Do you think we've spent enough time down here?" I asked the others quietly.

"I think if you spend any more time here, Dr. Yelton is going to track you down," Vincent said.

It felt awkward talking to Vincent, which had never happened before. "You're probably right. Rider, you're going with us."

"I'm not sure what the plan is," Vincent said. "Should I be going up with you all?"

"No," I said a little too quickly. "Just the injured."

"Then, I'll stay down here with Logan and catch up with you all later."

Seeing Dr. Yelton was one of the last things I wanted to do, but with the awkwardness with Vincent behind me, and Rider and Boone by my side, I trooped upstairs to get it over with.

Rider and Boone got off lucky. Dr. Yelton ordered some tests and sent them off with a nurse, all so that he could focus on me.

"Okay, Ms. Heidrich," Dr. Yelton said as we settled into a room in the clinic, "let's take a look at that arm. Walk me through what happened."

"I was shot in the arm," I said as he pinned up the sleeve of my dressing gown and began to unwind the bandage. "The bullet didn't go all the way through."

"Which hospital were you taken to? I can request the records."

"Um... There was no hospital. Not really anyway."

He inspected my arm carefully. "No hospital? Where were you? Let's start from the beginning."

"I'm not supposed to say."

"You don't have to be exact, but you've obviously received treatment. I need the details."

"We were in the middle of nowhere. It took a few days to get to an extraction point. By that time, my arm was infected. There was an... incident." I guess you can call dying an incident. I was worried about leaving that part out. It seemed like relevant medical information, but I couldn't say the words. "I had to use my abilities and pushed myself too far, so I was unconscious for a while."

"Do you know how long?"

"Not really. There are parts I don't remember, but when I woke up, Dr. Taylor was there. He had already removed the bullet."

"You saw him because...?"

"We were still pretty much in the middle of nowhere. My grandmother sent him to find us." I left out Fenrir. I wasn't about to mention a creature of the Path to AIR.

"Remarkable woman," Dr. Yelton said, with feeling.

"She is," I agreed. "Still, Dr. Taylor couldn't completely get rid of the infection with what he had. It wasn't until we reached a military installation that he could do enough to clear it up."

"I'll be sure to get his notes, but I trust his work. Now, I'm sending you to get an MRI. And we'll be able to get you started on physical therapy today."

Inwardly, I groaned at the idea of physical therapy. "How long until I can get the use of my arm back?"

"Dr. Taylor didn't tell you?"

"He wasn't sure."

"Well, let's see what your test results tell you and maybe I can give you an idea."

There's nothing worse than having to walk around the clinic in a hospital gown. It felt too much like being half-naked at work. Still, there weren't many people around, so when I left the room for tests my embarrassment was minimal.

By the time I was back with Dr. Yelton, Boone and Rider had already been cleared and left the clinic. I thought I'd be on my own.

I was so wrong.

The director knocked on the door. Her lips were pursed into a hard line. I'm not sure I'd ever seen her as stressed as she looked at that moment, even when Washington was breathing down her neck after our previous director tried to kill me.

"I'm checking in to see if we have some results. I understand you've already released the other agents," Kyrian said.

Dr. Yelton looked at me and I shrugged. She was going to hear the results anyway.

"I was just going over those. Since there are no objections, you can join us." Dr. Yelton consulted his tablet, keeping his concentration on the images on the screen. "Looks like you're healing nicely. Overall, it should only take a few more weeks until you get real use of your arm. Maybe a month. Physical therapy, however, will take longer. We'll start off slow. You should be able to start back to work in four to five weeks, at least on desk duty."

It felt like a punch in the stomach. "I have to be off work for a month?"

"You shouldn't be using your arm," Dr. Yelton said, "except for physical therapy."

"I have my sling. It's not like I'm throwing stuff around when I'm in the field."

"No, but you do get thrown around, and running is out of the question right now."

"What if she doesn't use the arm?" Kyrian asked.

"There's always a chance in the field," Dr. Yelton said, looking uncomfortable. "Even at the office, there's a chance—"

"May we speak in private for a few minutes, Dr. Yelton?" Kyrian asked.

The doctor mirrored my own confusion.

"Of course," the doctor said, rising. "Let's step over to my office. That will give Agent Heidrich a chance to get dressed."

As soon as they left the room, I eased the dressing gown off and redressed. For more than five minutes, I wandered around the room, looking for something of interest while I waited for them to return.

Dr. Yelton arrived alone, looking aggravated. "It seems there are special circumstances involved at this time."

"I'm going back to work?"

"As long as you follow my rules—*to the letter*—you will be allowed to take on work, part time." He didn't sound happy about it, but I was thrilled.

"What rules?"

"No lifting, that one should be obvious. No running, no jarring movements of any kind. You'll do nothing to put yourself in front of anyone that might need to be detained for any reason. Except for when performing the exercises I give you and when washing, your arm remains in that sling."

"I can manage that," I said. "Making house calls to the Lost shouldn't require any of that."

"No horseback riding," he added quickly. "And no ATVs. Someone else took over meeting with Essy while you were gone. That will continue."

"Can we make the no horseback riding permanent?"

Dr. Yelton smiled, but it was brief. "I think the director has an assignment for you. Since your skills are invaluable on this type of case, you can return to work. But if you break any of my rules, you're out of the field."

"What kind of case?" I asked.

"I don't know, but to keep you from doing anything, the director has agreed to give you an assistant in the field."

"An assistant?"

"Agent Boone is being assigned to your team for this case. It's the only reason I've agreed to this. If you'd rather have the time off, I'd be able to keep you off work."

It sounded like a last minute plea. "I'll be fine. I promise to stick to all your rules." Although I couldn't imagine anyone thinking that Boone was an assistant.

"Only four hours in the field each day," Dr. Yelton continued. "And at least one fifteen-minute break each hour."

"Okay," I said. Those weren't rules, right? I mean, he didn't say them before I agreed, so they must not count.

"Right," Dr. Yelton said, as though he read my mind and didn't hold out hope. "Let's go over your physical therapy."

He made me go over the exercises three times on my own before letting me leave the clinic.

When I made my way to the control room, I caught sight of Boone and Logan, and I joined them.

"I hear we have a case," I said as I approached.

"And a new partner," Logan said. "Kyrian thinks it'll be

easier to keep Boone here if he's put to work. It's supposed to keep us out of the fire as well."

"Do you really think the military will try to come down hard on us?"

Logan shrugged. "It's hard to say. I guess that depends on how much we say. We should mosey on down to the crime scene. They're holding the site for us."

I went to grab my bag, and Boone stepped in my way. "That's supposed to be my job," he said, grinning.

"Yeah, right."

"Take it up with the doctor if you want to complain," Boone said. "Let's go."

I didn't want anyone to see me break the rules before I even made it out of the office, so I let it go. "Where are Vincent and Rider?"

"Vincent needs to wrap up a few things," Logan said. "Rider's helping him out."

"What does he need to take care of?" I asked

"He walked between the worlds and was out of the office for weeks," Logan said. "He's got a mountain of paperwork to deal with. They'll catch up to us at the site."

On the way to the crime scene, I messed around with my new phone. Hank sent us case details, what few we had, and I read them out loud.

"We don't have much. Looks like the police found an eviscerated body. The local police called it in to us. How does that even happen?"

"Does it say who called it in?" Logan asked.

"No." I read through the rest of the notes. "Oh, it's local. I didn't realize it was so close."

"I guess that tells us who we're looking for," Logan said.

"Yeah." It felt like pixies were flying in my stomach.

"You know the local police?" Boone asked.

"One of them," Logan said.

"I dated a detective for a few months recently." My mind was racing about what I should say when I saw Ethan. He and I had broken up because he couldn't get over the idea that Vincent and I shared a soul. Now, Vincent and I were seeing each other and would be working a case with him.

"Recently?" Boone asked.

My nose scrunched up. "We broke up the night before we were sent to the gremlin world."

"It's been a few months then," Boone said. "That won't be too bad."

I disagreed, but kept that to myself.

"What makes this a case that we'd be called in on?" Logan asked.

"Nothing in the case file." I flipped back to the email that Hank sent. "But Hank said there was a witness that we may be interested in hearing."

"That's it?" Logan asked. "Kyrian must be dead set on getting us back to work."

"She's right, though," Boone said. "It might stall things."

"But stall what?" I asked. "Besides not checking in the first time we had a chance, we've done nothing wrong. Right?"

"Three military officers died during an AIR mission," Boone said. "We survived, they didn't. At the very least there's going to be an investigation."

"The military tried to kill us," I said, as if we needed the reminder. "Won't they want to sweep this under the carpet?"

"It could go two ways," Boone said. "Either it'll be a short investigation, open and shut, or they'll want to keep us quiet and we get arrested."

I've been in this position before. It was only a few months ago when the threat of being arrested loomed over my head. It was not a fun experience, so I decided to do what I did best. I ignored it.

Minutes later, we arrived on site as the sun was setting. At least where everyone was parked, anyway. We flashed our badges and found a place where the truck would fit in the crowded parking lot.

Logan approached the first officer he ran into. The man

shrugged at the badge and waved us over to someone else. Still, no sign of Ethan.

"Howdy," Logan said, approaching the officer indicated.

I lagged behind while Logan chatted. It hadn't been that long ago that people had a bad reaction to meeting me. One officer went so far as pulling a gun on me. That was fixed now, in theory, but I didn't want to push my luck.

When the officer finally waved us on, we had to trek through the park.

"You up for this?" Logan asked me.

"Why wouldn't I be?" It was a stupid thing to say; my nerves were a jangled mess.

"It's not too far a walk," Logan said, "but it's damned cold out here. I'm sure before the doc let you out of the clinic, he mentioned something about activity."

Logan might have been giving me something else to think about, besides seeing Ethan, but it was hard to say. "I'm not running, and Boone won't let me carry anything. Dr. Yelton didn't say anything about walking. No horses though."

"Good to know," Logan said, grinning.

We found our crime scene behind a large clump of trees.

I saw Ethan and my insides knotted up. He met us halfway to where the body lay on the ground.

"Logan, Cassie, it's good to see you again," Ethan said, all business, but with a few nervous glances at me. "And you are?"

"This is Agent Boone," Logan said. "Vincent and Rider will be along shortly."

Ethan looked around. "Thanks for coming in on this. I wouldn't have called you, but there's a few oddities that tell me the case might be one of yours."

"Oddities are our specialty," Logan said.

Although Ethan looked almost as nervous as I felt, he was starting to catch Logan's smile. "My team is finished with the site, so I'm sending the rest of them back. The witness is also back at the parking lot. We don't want to keep him longer than we have to." Ethan gestured to the two officers nearby.

"We'll take a quick look here, and then we'll go talk with him," Logan said.

To the officers, Ethan said, "Go ahead and let them know someone wants to talk to the witness in a few minutes."

They left, leaving us alone at the scene.

"Here's what we know," Ethan said, leading the way toward the body. "The victim is Gerald Mills. We're still confirming, but we think he cut through the park on his way home from work. Our witness was in the parking lot when he heard a scream."

It was starting to get dark. As we approached the body, Boone rummaged in our bag, pulled out a few flashlights, and passed one over to Logan. He hesitated before handing one to me.

I raised an eyebrow at him. "It's a flashlight. It weighs almost nothing."

He shrugged and handed it over.

Ethan's eyes lingered on my arm, still in its sling, but he continued. "The witness ran this way, but didn't hear anything else. The scream stopped before our witness left the parking lot."

"Easy to see why," Logan said somberly.

My nose curled up and I pursed my lips. I had to force myself to see the grisly scene in front of me. The man's insides weren't inside anymore.

"There appears to be only one cut," Ethan said. "Whatever it was it was sharp, but we'll know more after the autopsy."

I moved my flashlight to inspect the man's hands and face, avoiding the area where his intestines appeared to be on display.

"The witness rounded the trees, the same way you all came in," Ethan continued. "This is where things get weird. The witness described seeing a large thing with horns and a leathery face. It was leaning over the body, and it ran away when it saw the witness."

"Did he think it was an animal?" I asked.

"At first, he thought it was, but then assumed it was a tall man in a mask because it ran away on two legs, not four," Ethan said.

"But you don't think it was a man in a mask?" Logan asked.

"I was inclined to believe him, but then we found this." Ethan led us a short way from the body. The spot was bare earth, and imprinted in the ground, was the shape of what looked like a cloven hoof. "It looks like a footprint of some kind, but we can't be sure. We've been unable to identify what could have left it."

A cold chill that had nothing to do with the weather made its way down my spine. The track was the size of a small plate.

"It could be nothing, but I thought I'd call you all just in case," Ethan said.

"We'll look into it," Logan said. "Let's go talk to your witness, and we can check for more tracks as well."

The idea of walking back and forth across the park all night didn't sound like fun.

Logan must have sensed my feelings on the matter. "Cassie, why don't you stay here and see what you can see. Boone and I can handle the interview."

Boone seemed to hesitate.

"I'll stick around out here and wait for the ME. If you could let an officer know to send her my way, I'd appreciate it," Ethan said.

Once Logan and Boone disappeared behind the trees, I started to search the area for more evidence.

"So," Ethan said, his awkwardness palpable, "what happened to your arm?"

Ethan didn't like seeing me hurt on the job. It had been a touchy subject between us when we had been dating.

"I was shot," I said as though ripping off the bandage. "Our last case was a rough one." Rough was an understatement, but I wouldn't go into that with Ethan.

Or anyone else for that matter.

"How is everyone else?"

Another area of contention between us. I was often hurt when my partners weren't. Still, I managed to keep the aggravation out of my voice. Since there was a possibility that Ethan and I would be working together, I needed to let him know about Vincent and me.

"Boone ended up with a concussion, but it was over a week ago. He's okay now. Rider was stabbed, but you know him—he was okay the next day. Unfortunately, there were others on our team that didn't make it back." My chest seemed to tighten as I remembered the fact that I had killed one of them.

Ethan was quiet for a few moments, the atmosphere softening. "I'm so sorry to hear that."

"Thank you." I wasn't sure what else to say. After a few more moments of silence, I broached the subject that I'd been hoping to avoid. "It may be a little awkward working together."

"No," Ethan said. "It's good to see you again."

I plunged on. "But since we are working together, I wanted you to know up front that Vincent and I started seeing each other recently." I thought about last night. "Sort of anyway."

He didn't say anything for a few moments.

This was such an uncomfortable subject that I wish I had just avoided it all together. "It just happened. I promise that we were not together in any way while you and I were together." I could feel my face turn red.

"I know you weren't," Ethan said.

Out of the corner of my eye, I saw him wearing a half smile. It looked sad, but it was there.

"It's good that you two are together."

I looked up and raised an eyebrow at him in disbelief.

"It is," he said, and he sounded sincere. "I think it's good that you two give what you have a shot. Don't feel bad because of me."

"It's going to be a little weird." I hated to press it, but I wanted to be honest.

"It doesn't need to be. I'm glad you're happy. Thank you for telling me, though. I appreciate it."

We both moved around the area in silence for a while, flashlights working hard to burn away the cold darkness that seemed to be pushing in.

The sound of a vehicle approaching came from the other side of the clump of trees.

"Someone's driving back here?" I asked.

"Not all the way," Ethan said, "but it'll be easier to bring the victim out this way. They might need to heat the area up some before moving him."

"I didn't think of that," I said, scrunching my nose up.

"It's not below freezing yet, but it feels like it's getting close."

The truck stopped and I could hear people approaching. I was surprised when I heard Rider and Vincent's voices.

My stomach tightened once again. All was well and good for Ethan to say he was okay with Vincent and me, but was he really fine with it?

Vincent and Rider rounded the corner, and Ethan went to

meet them. I wandered in that direction still watching the ground, but intent on hearing what they said.

"Rider, Vincent, it's good to see you again," Ethan said. Once again, he sounded sincere. Ethan shook Rider's hand and then held it out for Vincent.

Most people wouldn't have noticed, but I knew Vincent well enough to see that he hesitated before grasping Ethan's proffered hand.

"It is good to see you," Rider said. "I think your medical examiner is on her way."

"Do you need to see anything before they take the body away?" Ethan asked.

Vincent shook his head.

"I do not," Rider said. "There are a lot of smells to sort through, but the victim's is very distinguishable."

Rider started circling the body.

"Isn't Boone supposed to be sticking to you?" Vincent asked.

I rolled my eyes. "I'm holding a flashlight and walking around. I'm not exactly overexerting myself." As I said it, I did notice the dull ache that was starting to form in my arm, but I ignored it.

Vincent grinned for a moment before his face went blank once again. It may have been just me, but he seemed to be disinclined to come any closer to me.

"Do I want to trace the victim or the attacker?" Rider said.

"We have an idea of where the victim came from," I said. "It would be good to get a better idea of where the suspect went after he left here."

Rider nodded. "There have been a lot of people in the area, but there is one smell that is not familiar. Part of that smell seems to be blending with that of another human's. It is odd."

"Is the new smell one of the Lost?" I asked.

Rider shrugged. "It is from a race or species with which I am unfamiliar. I cannot say for sure whether it is Lost or something from this world that I do not know."

"In this area, I'm betting on Lost," Vincent said. "With all the hiking and stuff you all do, you've probably run into everything indigenous."

"That is possible," Rider said.

Three people I didn't know walked around the corner, two pulling a piece of equipment that looked like a stretcher, but the bed was hard and sunken like a bowl. Ethan went to meet them."

"Cass, are you reading the area?"

"No, just checking for prints and stuff."

"Boone and Logan?" Vincent asked.

"Talking to a witness. I'm sure they'll be back soon."

"If you're okay here, we'll catch up to you all later then." Vincent turned to Rider. "Let's see where this person might have gone."

The two disappeared into the night.

"Should we follow them?" Ethan asked.

"They are walking past the print you found," I said. "It might not hurt to walk that way a little."

We started in that direction and I looked around. I could hear cars back out on the road, but I couldn't see them. There were no lights. It was by no means dark with the light pollution of our little city, but the trees in the area obscured any direct light.

"Did the victim have his wallet?" I asked, shining my light into the nearest clump of trees.

"He did," Ethan said. "He was also still wearing his watch."

"Since the suspect was seen leaning over the body, it could be that he was interrupted before he was able to take them. It sounded like he had plenty of time before the witness arrived, though."

"Could be. We have officers talking with his friends and coworkers. So far, we haven't seen anything that would cause him specifically to become a target. It's too early to tell, though."

My mind spun, trying to make sense of the situation. Why would a Lost kill some random person, if not for theft?

"Are you, um, doing your thing?" Ethan asked.

"Reading? No. I'm just looking." My breathing increased at the thought of reading. The last time I used my powers, I died. It had been almost two weeks since I even thought about stepping into the Path.

CHAPTER

FOUR

Ethan's radio squawked to life, and he stepped away to talk. Searching the ground by flashlight seemed fruitless. It was dark, cold, and I didn't really expect to find anything. If there were anything physical, Rider and Vincent would spot it. Looking back, I could see the silhouette of the body being taken away.

I headed back to the main scene and Ethan fell into step.

"The witness has been sent home," Ethan said.

Sure enough, Logan and Boone met us back at the crime scene. Flags still littered the ground, but the body was gone.

"Find anything new?" Logan asked.

"Nothing," I said.

"Vincent sent me a text," Logan said. "They should be back any minute."

Logan and Boone looked over the site as well. Boone concentrated on the clump of trees while Logan scoured the ground, much as I had done.

When Vincent and Rider walked out of the darkness, we joined them.

"I was unable to track the smell very far," Rider said, looking disappointed.

"It's not your fault," Vincent said. To us, he added, "The trail led to the street a few blocks away and disappeared. It's possible the person we were trailing got a ride, or..."

"Or what?" I asked.

"There was some broken glass on the ground," Vincent said. "Safety glass. It's possible a vehicle was stolen or something."

"Was it right where the trail disappeared?" Logan asked.

"Yes," Rider said.

"You could be right." Logan looked around and waved Ethan over. "Have you heard anything about a missing car in the area?"

"A car was reported stolen a few hours ago," Ethan said. "We're looking into it since it was so close to the scene."

"Can you send us the information?" Logan asked.

"Sure. I'll have it sent right over."

Logan turned back to Vincent and Rider. "Why don't you two take a look around in case we missed something? Another set of eyes won't hurt."

"I'll show you the things we've marked off," Ethan said.

I watched the three wander back over to where the body had been found. I wasn't at all sure how Vincent was feeling with Ethan around. My arm was sore, which was starting to make me cranky and could have contributed to my inability to read Vincent. It could also have been my own anxiety over having Ethan and Vincent in close range getting in my way. They were too far away now for me to hear what they were saying.

"I don't suppose you got a read on the area?" Logan asked.

The suggestion make my heart leap into my throat. "I haven't."

"Do you want to check it out?" Logan asked.

It was hard to catch my breath. My gaze was drawn to Vincent, who took two steps in my direction before glancing at Ethan and stopping. Ethan watched Vincent, knowing that Vincent would respond if something were wrong with me. I really hoped Ethan didn't assume Vincent sensed my intense anxiety. I turned away from them, so only Logan and Boone could see my face, which I tried to keep passive.

"I haven't tried to open the Path since South America," I said, keeping my voice low.

"Want to give it a shot?" Logan asked.

My mind screamed 'No!' as loud as it could. "I can try." I wanted to look around to make sure the others weren't watching, but doing that advertised my discomfort to the world.

Instead, I closed my eyes, took a few deep breaths, and stretched myself to the edge of my mind. Tentatively, I tried to jump into the Path.

It didn't come.

My fear began to melt into confusion. "Nothing happened."

Once again, I tried. My mind stood at the edge of an abyss and resolutely refused to move any further.

"It's not working." Frowning, I looked at Logan as though he might have an idea. "I couldn't reach the Path."

"It's been a long day," Logan said.

"Preceded by a few long weeks," Boone added.

"Not to mention your arm's busted up," Logan said.

They were trying to reassure me, but it wasn't working.

"I'll go see if they found anything we didn't." Logan made a quick escape.

Boone looked uncomfortable. "It's probably past time for you to take a break."

I rolled my eyes, but since my arm hurt and exhaustion was trying to drag me down, I didn't say anything.

"Let's head back to the truck," Boone said.

"Sure."

Ethan caught up to us as we rounded the trees. "It sounds like Logan and the others are wrapping up now."

"Thanks for calling us in," I said. "It was good timing for the team."

"Vincent didn't seem too happy about being out here," Ethan said.

Boone snorted. "I don't think I've seen him happy about being anywhere."

"That's not true." I'm not sure why I felt the need to defend Vincent, but I did all the same.

"I can never get a read off him to know one way or the other. It's getting colder," Ethan said, stumbling over the change in subject. "How's your arm holding up?"

"Not bad. I could do without the cold, though."

"It preserves the scene," Boone said. "That's the only good thing I can say about it."

"We'll keep it roped off for a few days," Ethan said. "Longer if you need it. And we'll have officers around the area for the next day or so."

"Thanks," I said as we neared the parking lot.

"I'll see you around," Ethan said. The parking lot was almost empty, but he waved over the few remaining officers.

We waited near the truck for the rest of the team, despite the cold. Ethan and Boone had been right about one thing. Vincent hadn't looked happy about working with Ethan. He didn't seem upset about it either. Worried maybe?

If that was the case, then I wanted to know sooner rather than later.

"So," Boone said as the others approached, "what do we think?"

"The witness seemed pretty convinced it was a person in a mask," Logan said. "But I think that's something they're telling themselves so they can sleep tonight. I think this is one of ours."

"I agree," Rider said. "The smell was too alien for the area."

"Unless a horned, goat-footed Lost is familiar to anyone, I think we need some research," Logan said. "Cassie's house, tomorrow morning?"

"That sounds good," Rider said, stifling a yawn.

We broke apart, but not before, I caught Vincent's eye.

"I'll call you," he said.

I nodded, still unable to get a read on him. He hadn't given me a chance to invite him over, but I could always do that when he called.

Boone decided to go home with Logan in order to check in with Renick. I could tell that Boone was interested in what Renick would be doing. As I dragged myself into the house, I reflected on the fact that it was strange to be around a man who had decided he wanted the world to consider him dead.

Although, it was possibly stranger to think that we went along with it, and were keeping the information from the outside world.

The house was quiet and dark. Though, it had been dark for hours, it still hadn't reached midnight. Gran was already in bed, so I quietly made my way to the kitchen to find something to eat.

Gran had left a bowl of stew for me and another one for Boone along with a note. I read the message while I heated my dinner.

. . .

There's dinner for you and Mr. Boone. Can you check on Molly before you go to bed? It would make me feel better if you did.

Love, Gran

I STOPPED the microwave before it beeped and set dinner aside. "Molly?" I called softly, not wanting to wake Gran. With no response, I called a little louder.

Sounds of movement stirred in the other room and Molly padded in from the living room with Gran's cat close on her heels. She sat and looked at me expectantly.

"How are you doing?" I moved to her and petted her with one hand and then scratched Gran's cat behind the ears. My cell phone rang, but I took another moment with Molly. "You look okay."

When I stood, Molly flung up her tail and traipsed out of the room. I answered my cell phone as I watched her leave.

"Hello," I said.

"Sorry to call so late."

Despite the strangeness from the previous night, Vincent's voice made me smile. "I'm glad you did. We didn't get a chance to talk much today."

"I should have called this morning, but not talking earlier was probably for the best."

"Why?" My smile couldn't be worn down.

"I should talk with Ethan first, if we're going to work with him."

It was thoughtful of him, and for a moment, I wished others saw this side of him. "I already let Ethan know. He's okay with it."

"Sure he is."

"No, I think he meant it. I mean, I doubt he's thrilled, but he understood and sounded sincere."

"I'll talk with him anyway."

After a few beats of silence, I felt the need to fill the void. "Do you want to talk about last night?"

There was a long heavy silence on Vincent's end, followed by caution. "If we need to."

My good mood faltered. "Need to?"

"It won't happen again." His voice was monotone, and I wished we were in the same room so I would at least have a chance to know how he was feeling.

"I'm still not sure..." I struggled with what to say. "I mean, I was having a bad dream."

"And you woke up to a worse one."

It was my turn to be silent. *What could be worse than what I dream?*

Hurting Vincent while I was asleep. That would be worse.

"I'm sorry," Vincent said when I was quiet for too long. He sounded as though his walls dropped, at least a little. "I shouldn't have fallen asleep."

"Of course you should have," I said. "I didn't mean to..."

"Don't apologize for something I did."

"That you did? You mean I didn't... I mean, I thought I used my power and pushed you or something."

"Why would you think that?"

I bit my lip, and then threw out what I was afraid of. "In my dream, I threw Davis, and then I woke up and you were on the floor."

He was quiet. "That's not what happened. I grabbed your arm. The moment I realized I had you, I jerked back and fell out of bed."

"You're sure?"

"I am."

I wasn't convinced, but I felt a little better about it.

"You know what happened in the jungle wasn't your fault," Vincent said.

Not a direction I wanted the conversation to go. "Sure. Listen, it's late. I'll let you go."

"We should talk about this."

I tried to make sure my voice was light. "We can talk tomorrow."

"Do you want me to come over?"

The worry I heard made me feel guilty. "Of course I do, but tomorrow will be better. I'll see you in the morning."

I ate a few bites of stew before storing the rest and heading to bed. Boone had a key, so I wasn't worried about waiting for him to get back. Careful of my arm, I showered and went through the exercises that Dr. Yelton gave me. By the time I was done, my arm burned like fire. The idea of taking a pain pill crossed my mind. It wasn't exactly ideal, but in the end, I decided a good night's sleep would make up for the possible drowsiness in the morning.

Even with the medication running through me, I tossed and turned for a while, spending way too much time worried about what Vincent was thinking.

The whole conversation played itself out in my mind, and the whole gamut of emotions trickled through. Had I been too pushy? Moving too fast? Maybe he was looking for something more physical, and less...close?

I had assumed a deep connection between Vincent and myself, but I had no idea if he felt the same way. The fire that flared between us was definitely physical. Even if that's all we had, it wasn't a bad place to start.

I OPENED my eyes and blinked at the dark ceiling. Something had woken me. My sluggish mind was trying to pinpoint what it was when I heard a loud shriek from downstairs.

My chest seized and I jumped out of bed. I was halfway across the room when I realized I didn't have my gun. Luckily, it was nearby, and I snagged it and ran down the stairs. With my heart beating fast, I ripped my arm out of the sling as I reached the first floor. A screech unlike anything I had ever heard filled the house. It was a siren. An alarm.

I flipped on the lights and held my gun out, sweeping the living room, then rushed to the kitchen where the sound became a rumbling anger.

My arm protested when I reached automatically for the switch, but the light spilling in from the living room illuminated everything I needed to see.

The creature was enormous. Brown lumpy skin covered the stocky towering frame. It wore clothes of a sort, but the material looked rough and was like nothing I had ever seen. These things my mind could take in. I could comprehend them.

Two large horns like that of a ram curled out of the monster's forehead. Marks on the ceiling bore witness to the fact the beast could barely fit into the room. It had a muzzle of sorts with sharp jagged teeth that protruded from his dark mouth. That wasn't what stopped me dead. The enormity of what I was seeing wouldn't sink in.

The person appeared to unfreeze, which gave it an advantage over me. It grunted and drew back, shaking its leg along the way.

That was when I saw Molly. She had fastened herself to the creature and torn a large chunk out of its leg. Blood soaked her fur.

The creature bellowed at me, turned, and ran. The door behind it was shut, but it didn't seem overly concerned about it. It appeared to be such a minor inconvenience as it crashed through. It might as well have not been an obstacle.

Finally, realizing I had legs and could move, I rushed to the door. The night air sucked any warmth out of the room. The creature had managed to dislodge Molly, but she looked as though she were still ready for a fight. She called out her alarm into the dark yard, and I sunk down to the ground next to her to look her over.

There was so much blood. In her agitated state, I didn't dare try to touch her.

"Molly," I said, trying to keep my voice calm. "Are you okay?"

Molly howled, and I felt tears sting my eyes. "Good girl. You scared him off. He didn't get far…" I looked into the other room. Gran hadn't stirred.

My bare feet slipped in blood as I forced myself to my feet. "Gran!" My arm burned, but it was background noise as I raced through the living room and barged into Gran's room. Gran stood on the other side of her bed, gun in hand, aimed straight at me.

I stopped, but only for a moment. It was a horrifying real-ization that that monster could have reached her. Sobbing, I ran around the bed and hugged her.

"You're okay, hun," Gran said. "We both are. It's okay now."

Even if I wanted to respond, I couldn't have at the moment. It was as though I'd stopped breathing in my rush to Gran's room, and now my lungs were punishing me for it. That wasn't easy while I was crying.

Gran patted my back. "Is Molly okay?" The strained worry in her voice was the only thing that could have moved me.

"She is," I lied, I didn't really know for sure. "I'll go check on her. Stay here and keep your gun on you."

Trembling, I stepped out of the room. Peeking around the

corner, I saw that the living room was empty. My bloody foot-prints marred the carpet, but I'd have to worry about that later. I padded into the kitchen and found Molly still by the door. She looked calmer, but on guard.

I sat back down, avoiding the blood this time, and called out to her. It took some coaxing, but after a few tries, she stalked over to me and began to sniff.

"Cassie?" Logan called from outside the house.

Molly tensed as the elf bounded in. She hissed at the sudden movement, but then ignored us both to stand sentry by the door.

"Is the house clear?" Logan asked, his gun was in hand, and he was keeping an eye trained on the living room.

"Yeah, it's gone."

"Shit!" Boone cursed. He carefully went around Molly.

"Margaret?" Logan asked.

"She's okay. I checked on her."

"Where are you hurt?" Boone grabbed a towel and dropped down beside me.

"I'm not," I said, snatching the towel before he could start mopping up the blood on my feet and legs. "I'm just..." I waved my hand towards the door, trying to indicate my frustrations with the world at large. When words failed me, I shifted gears. "Cold. I'm just cold."

"Is Molly okay?" Gran asked, peeking into the room.

"She is," I said, scrambling to my feet again.

"Boone and I are going to clear the house," Logan said.

Boone took one last look over Gran and me, and then followed Logan.

"This place looks..." Gran stopped and shook her head. "I think I need a drink."

I could have used some hard liquor, as well, but I didn't say it. Had this really happened? I'd only been home for a few days, and already my job had threatened my family again.

This was something I needed to approach carefully with Gran. "Don't worry. I'll get this cleaned up. Why don't you stay at Mom's for a few days?"

"Nothin' is gonna chase me out of my home. Besides, Molly's here to keep us safe."

Molly looked up at the sound of her name, but quickly went back to peering into the darkness of the night.

"Of course not, but it may take a while to get the door fixed. Molly can save us from monsters, but it's going to get cold down here." Frigid was more like it. I wasn't sure if the blood was drying on my skin or freezing there. "It might be good to stay with Mom for a few days."

"If I show up to see her at this time in the morning, both of us are never gonna hear the end of it."

I hadn't thought about it that way. "That's true."

"Still, it's not a bad idea. How long does it take to get a door?"

"I think getting the door is easy. Getting it installed and getting the damage fixed may take a while."

"Where will you stay?"

"I thought I might stay with Vincent," I lied.

Gran grinned. "That will work out fine. Tell you what. Why don't we get this hole plugged up, and I can stay in Vincent's room tonight. It should stay warm enough up there."

"I'll get Logan and Boone to help me with this. It's work related, so it's our mess. Why don't you take Molly with you and go on upstairs? She's going to catch a cold if she stays down here all night."

"You take care of the door and I'll get Molly cleaned up," Gran said. "And then we can both still get some sleep."

It took a while to coax Molly away from her post, but Gran managed it. As they left the room, I stared at the ruined door and tried to figure out what to do next.

"The house is clear," Logan said as he and Boone returned. "Why don't you tell us what happened here?"

"Work followed me home."

"This was work?"

"It's always work." I tried to keep the leaden depression from my voice, but it was no use. "This… thing—what our witness saw tonight. Horns and all. And I can tell you, it wasn't a man in a mask." I pointed to the ceiling by way of explanation.

"I'll call it in," Logan said. "Hank can arrange to have the mess fixed up tomorrow morning. Go get cleaned up before you freeze to death. We'll get started processing the scene."

"Why did this happen here?" I hadn't meant to ask the question, but it came out anyway.

"What do you mean?" Logan asked.

"Why here? Why does this happen in my house?"

Logan's forehead wrinkled in confusion. "Look at this from the outside. If a suspect is trying to get to one of us for whatever reason, what does he see when he looks at us? An elf, a werewolf, a Walker, and a Reader. If they know anything about our world, they're going to know what to expect from the rest of us. No one outside the team really knows what you do. You're also the only woman on the team. They may think that's to their advantage."

"I'm the weakest link."

Logan shrugged. "From the outside, that's how it looks. It's our luck they're wrong."

I raised a skeptical eyebrow at him.

He grinned. "Go get cleaned up. We'll get started down here."

CLEANUP WENT SLOWLY. Mostly because Boone stayed true to his word of not letting me do anything. Once I showered and put on warmer clothes, my arm was back in its sling and I was banished to the sidelines while they gathered what they could from the scene. They had plenty of blood samples.

Logan managed to put the largest piece of the door roughly back into its place. Boone fastened blankets to the wall to stem the flow of wind through the gaps, and at six in the morning, they were on their way to the home improvement store.

Mom picked Gran up early. Thankfully, she didn't make it inside the house. It was a relief to have Gran somewhere safer, even though she wouldn't take Molly with her. She swore up and down that there was no way Mom was going to let a cat in her house, much less an animal like Molly.

For a short while, I was left alone in the house. Molly

prowled around once again. She never stayed in one room long, and for some reason, she even patrolled the second floor.

I put the time to use and began to scrub my bloody footprints from the floor. The carpet was a disaster, all the way through the living room and into Gran's room. Feeling guilty about Gran's experience, I started in her room. It wasn't easy with only one hand to scrub, but at least I felt useful.

The doorbell rang a little after seven. Figuring it was Boone and Logan back with supplies, I called out for them to come in, something I'd never do if Gran had been there.

There was quiet in the other room. Figuring I was going to be banished from work by Boone again, I scrubbed a particularly large spot of blood.

"Cass?" called Vincent from the other room.

"Crap." I scrambled to my feet and hurried out of Gran's room.

Frowning, Vincent looked me over. This close, I could feel his emotions churning beneath the surface.

"Is everyone okay?"

"We're fine, the house not so much."

His brow furrowed deeper, so I gestured towards the kitchen.

He stood in the entry and stared at the blankets on the wall and the blood on the floor. "What—" he started, and then stopped. He seemed to be having a hard time, so I grabbed a cup of coffee and filled him in on the night's excitement.

"Why wasn't Boone here?" Vincent asked, keeping his voice level.

"What?" My mind was running a little slow from lack of sleep. "I don't know. I didn't ask."

"He should have been here." There was a steel edge to his voice.

"What?" It didn't sound any better the second time, but

the question lit embers of anger. "He can come and go as he wants. He's a guest, not a guard."

"I should have been here." The steel grew sharper

I worked to keep my voice softer. "It's not your job to be here either."

"How did I not know about this?"

"Once it was over, it was over. I figured I would fill you in today and didn't see a reason to bother you last night."

"You should have called, but that's not what I meant. I should have known. Something like this... You could have been killed. I should have sensed it."

"Isn't that only if you're close? I can only tell how you're feeling when I see you, and even then it's hard."

"No. Not for me. I was only across town. Yesterday, when you were upset, I knew."

"Last night, you were asleep across town."

He didn't say anything for a while. "You're sure you're okay? And Margaret?"

"We're fine. I promise."

"Where is she?"

"I asked her to go to Mom's for a few days."

His emotions were roiling beneath the surface. I wasn't sure what to do, so I waited it out. Moments slowly ticked by.

Vincent moved over to me, took my cup of coffee out of my hand and sat it on the counter. Then he embraced me. While carefully avoiding my arm, he drew as close to me as he could. His warmth soaked into me, and our energies merged. I pressed into him. Despite the fatigue of the night, Vincent caused quite the effect. More than ever, I wanted my arm out of its sling and back to normal.

He pulled back enough to look me in the eyes, studying me. His lips touched mine, and my toes curled. I could tell that I wasn't the only one responding to our closeness. When our breathing increased, he pulled back and put his hand on my cheek.

"Will you call me next time?" Vincent asked. "If there is a next time?"

"If there's a next time? Have you seen my track record?"

A hint of a grin peeked out. "Yes, but you just made it harder to get rid of me."

Maybe there was a silver lining to last night.

"Where is everyone?" he asked, not pulling away.

"Home improvement store. They should be back soon."

He looked behind him at the blankets. "Let's take a look at the damage."

It was hard not to sigh sadly when he stepped away. The loss of warmth was immediate, and I missed the feeling of his body pressed into mine. Still, Logan and Boone would be back soon.

Vincent pulled back the blanket and looked surprised by what he saw. "It would take a raging minotaur to cause this much damage." He shifted something, and I heard wood clatter to the ground. "It looks like a rhino smashed through."

"It was big." I caught myself and realized I had been doing that all night. "He, I mean. He was big."

"He?"

"I don't think he was female, and whatever else he might be, he's intelligent. He quietly let himself into the house, so we aren't dealing with an animal."

"Why did he target you?"

"I'm just that lucky."

Vincent dropped the blanket. "No, really. Why come all the way out here? My apartment is closer to where he was last seen."

"Logan thinks it's because I'm human and female, which makes me appear to be the easiest target."

"But why come after any of us?" Vincent asked. "It's not like we're closing in on a suspect."

"We don't even have a way of tracking him unless he stays on foot."

"It doesn't make sense unless we have something he wants. He broke in. I wonder if he was planning on stealing something."

"Luckily, he didn't know about Molly," I said.

Vincent grinned. "Even if he had seen Molly, I doubt he would have expected her to be a guard. Much less an effective one."

At the sound of her name, Molly once again trotted into the room.

Vincent crouched down next to her and scratched her behind the ears. "Good girl."

My smile grew watching them. They looked cute together. Molly rubbed up against him before making her way around the room and leaving once again.

"I was hoping Gran would take Molly with her," I said, "but she didn't think Mom would like it."

"Do you think someone might be after Margaret?"

"Not really, but I'd feel better if she had something other than her gun for protection."

"I thought she was getting rid of the gun."

"She was holding it when I went to her room to check on her. I'm pretty sure she carries it around in her purse."

There was a knock on the front door.

"It's us," called Logan as it opened.

"We're in here," I said.

"We picked up everything," Logan said, "but we're going to have to unload it and go. Hank just called. Another body's been found."

"Is it safe to leave the house with a giant hole in it?" I asked.

"I thought we'd get Boone to hang around here," Logan said. "He hasn't been to sleep yet, anyway."

"I'm good to go with you," Boone said.

"We don't even know if it's related," Logan said. "Cool your heels here. We'll be back before you know it."

It took very little time for Logan to unload the supplies. Once he did, the three of us were off, leaving Boone back at the house.

"Howdy," Logan said, walking up to where Ethan and Rider, who had beaten us to the scene, were chatting. "What do we have?

"Twenty-one-year-old female," Ethan said. "We don't have any witnesses, but the wounds are fairly consistent, so I thought we'd call you in."

"There are two smells at this site that match the crime scene from yesterday," Rider said.

"Two?" I asked. "Do we have two people working together on this?"

"Two smells are very similar," Rider said. "I cannot be certain that they do not belong to the same person."

"Can a person smell more than one way?" Ethan asked.

"People and animals have a base smell," Rider said. "They also have other smells that blend and affect the base. Hormones, pheromones, foods, hygiene, it can all affect the smell."

"Do you have an estimated time of death?" Logan asked.

"Between two and four this morning," Ethan said.

"If we're dealing with the same guy, it'd have to be closer to four," Logan said.

"What makes you say that?" Ethan asked.

"Our suspect gave Cassie a little visit this morning," Logan said. "It was almost three when he was chased away."

Worry washed over Ethan's face. He looked to me, then to Vincent. Though Vincent had been keeping his distance from me, he shifted closer.

"Everyone okay?" Ethan asked.

"We're fine," I said. "But he was bleeding pretty bad when he left."

When I turned to Rider, I found him much closer than he had been previously. He tried to be unobtrusive about it, but I was pretty sure he was smelling me.

"Can you tell if he was still bleeding here?" I asked Rider.

Rider walked around me, forcing others back, and then he did the same to Logan. "I do not smell blood here, but I am not familiar with this Lost, so it is possible that I am smelling it but not recognizing it. There is some trace of smell on you that is also here."

"If he was at my house and over here within an hour, wouldn't he still be bleeding?" I asked. "Molly tore into him pretty bad."

"There was a lot of blood on your floor," Logan said. "But until we know what type of Lost we're dealing with, it's hard to say if he would still be bleeding or not. Rider, have you checked the area already?"

Rider wrinkled his nose. "As far as I could. I am afraid another smell broke the trail."

"What do you mean?" Vincent asked.

"It would be like someone dropping a bottle of peppermint oil," Rider said. "There was a scent strong enough that it covered the other smells in the area."

"Do you reckon someone did that on purpose?" Logan asked.

Rider shrugged. "I do not know why someone would, but it is impossible to know."

"They might if they knew someone with a good sense of smell was after them," Vincent said.

"How would someone know something like that?" Ethan asked. "It's not like you advertise."

"There's a lot going on that doesn't seem to add up," Logan said. "Let's get what we can from here and get some research done. We need to find what it is we're dealing with."

"We need to get the body moved as soon as we can," Ethan said.

We took a quick look at the victim, but aside from knowing that her insides were outside, I couldn't tell much more by looking. And I wasn't too keen on checking too closely.

"We haven't found any other evidence yet," Ethan said. "I'll send you a copy of all we have."

Logan looked at me, and I knew he was going to ask me to read the area. Only...

He didn't.

CHAPTER
SIX

"Rider, let's take one last look around," Logan said. "Vincent and Cassie, why don't you get started on research? We'll meet you back at Cassie's house."

We waved goodbye to Ethan while he worked with a team to move the victim.

The wind picked up as Vincent and I got in the truck. Shivering, I cranked up the heat and stared out the window as Vincent wound his way through the streets.

Logan hadn't asked me to read the scene. The idea was lurking like a heavy toad in the forefront of my mind.

"Want to talk about it?" he asked.

"Talk about what?"

"You seem worried."

Normally, I'd want to keep this kind of thing to myself, or maybe talk with Rider about it, but I was probably making a big deal out of nothing. "Do you think it's strange that Logan didn't ask me to read the site?"

"No." The answer was immediate. "He asked you last night, didn't he?"

"Yeah." I shifted uncomfortably, not wanting to talk about yesterday's failure.

"That surprises me more than him not asking today."

"Why is that? It's my job."

Vincent took a while to reply, as though formulating his response. "Last time you used your powers, you died." His fingers strained on the steering wheel as he gripped harder while resolutely staring straight ahead. "You saved us all, but we almost lost you."

"That doesn't mean I can't do my job." To myself, I added, *unless I burned myself out.* Was that why I couldn't read last night?

"He knows that. We all know that, but I think… I think it's important to remember that what we do is dangerous. If we waste too much energy on something when we don't need it, it won't be there when we do."

"It's not a waste if it helps. It's what I do."

"It's not just you, it's all of us. Boone looks like he's half-dead today because he was up all night. He wasn't essential at the site today, but he might be this evening. We don't know what's going to happen, but it'll help us be better prepared if we work smarter."

"Have you all been discussing this?"

"We did while we were trying to get out of the rain forest."

"I hadn't used my powers the day the missiles dropped on us. There's nothing different we could have done."

"No, but you were injured and ill. If you had been over-worked on top of that, would we still be here?"

"It's possible, but I never thought about it. I try not to think about it."

"I know."

I couldn't imagine a world where I didn't use my powers on my job. "What will I do in the field if I don't use my gifts?"

"You'll use them when you want to, or when you need to. I'd like it if you waited until you were back to full strength, but I know that's not up to me. When you're not using them, you'll do the same as the rest of us. I don't use my skills unless I need to. I work the case."

"I guess I'm just so used to using them, it feels weird not to."

"No one's saying you can't use them. We're just saying you don't have to if you don't need to."

Even though the idea of not reading at a crime scene was uncomfortable, it felt good to have partners that would back me up, no matter what I decided to do.

Crisp air held the smell of snow when we got out of the truck at my house. I shoved my hand into my pocket and hurried to the door. However, before I could reach it, Vincent snagged my good arm and stopped me.

When I turned to him, he surprised me with a kiss. A current sparked between us. I put my good arm around him and let him pull me close. When he drew back slightly, I didn't want to let him go.

Vincent's smile lit up his face bright enough for the world to see. "I love that I get to do that now."

"Me too."

"I suppose we should get inside before we freeze to death."

"Really? I'm feeling plenty warm at the moment."

I kissed him again and could feel his smile. Still, the temperature was dropping and eventually, reluctantly, we pulled apart and made our way inside.

Boone was in the living room, sprawled out on the couch with his computer on his lap. It was nice to see that he was starting to get comfortable around the house.

When he saw us, though, he sat up.

"I thought you'd be asleep," I said, flopping down into a chair.

"I thought I'd get some research in," Boone said. "How were things on site?"

"Not great," I said. "It looks like the same person that killed the guy from yesterday. The same person that was here last night."

"I'm sorry about last night," Boone said. "I should have been here."

You're living here. You can come and go as you want," I chuckled. "Besides, if you want to be here every time someone breaks in, you may as well not even leave."

Boone looked at me, eyes raised. "Happen often? I thought last time must have been a fluke."

"More often than it should," I said.

"Once is too much," Vincent said.

"Anyway," I said. "We have Molly for protection."

"She's something else," Boone said. "I never expected something that small to do so much damage."

"She certainly does her job well," I agreed. "They say ichneu used to slay dragons. I can believe it after seeing her savage someone. Once she's grown, she'll be a force to be reckoned with."

"I thought I might get a place where Renick can also lay low, but it sounds like he may not need it," Boone said.

"Has he decided to come back from the dead?" I asked.

"No, but I talked with him last night. Margaret's boyfriend has been in touch with him, along with Cronos. He's going to be working for them, but he's not sure where he'll be."

"What's he doing?" Vincent asked.

"He wouldn't say. I got the idea that he wasn't too sure himself."

"What about you?" I asked. "They said they'd be talking with you as well."

"They haven't contacted me," Boone said. "We have enough trouble right now. News is filtering through the organization. Whoever tried to kill us is going to find out that they missed."

"They didn't miss," Vincent said.

"True," Boone said. "But it's probably better if they think they have. Better than the alternative."

"Good point," Vincent said.

"I guess we should get back to work," I said. "I'm going to go grab my laptop and check MyTH's files to see if they have anything on what we're looking for."

"Don't even think about it," Boone warned. "Your laptop is light, but not that light. Where is it? I'll get it for you."

"You don't have to—"

"It's my job." Boone grinned. "Remember?"

"They just said that to give you a better reason to stay on the team for now," I said.

"Where is it?" Boone asked, ignoring everything I had just said.

I sighed and slumped back in my chair. "On my desk in my room."

"Let's move to the kitchen table," Vincent said. "It'll be easier to work."

"More importantly, it's closer to the coffee."

I anticipated cold when I walked into the kitchen. While it wasn't as warm as the living room, it was still much warmer than I expected. The hole in the wall was still covered with a blanket, but when I pulled it back, I wasn't faced with currents of air directly from outside.

"I closed it up a little better when you were gone," Boone

said. "The door and frame should be the only things that need to be replaced."

"Thank you," I said. "This is great."

Boone put down my laptop and found somewhere to plug it in. "It's probably overkill, but I wasn't sure when someone would be out to repair it. Turns out, you have someone coming by this afternoon to get started. A cleaner should be here as well."

"Looks like you've already cleaned quite a bit," I said, noting the lack of blood on the floor.

"Only the kitchen. I have no idea what to do with the carpet, and I'd likely only make it worse."

"Thanks," I repeated. "I really appreciate all of this."

"Happy to help."

I needed a fresh injection of caffeine, so I made a pot of coffee. Out of the corner of my eye, I noticed Boone getting ready to make a comment while I filled the carafe with water. He wisely decided against saying anything. I needed to start carrying a little weight every now and again, right? It was bad enough my muscles in one arm were almost useless.

With a fresh cup of coffee in front of me, I started wading through the MyTH files. It wasn't long before Rider and Logan joined us. They brought lunch, which I hoped would be a welcomed break. Instead, we ended up quietly researching as we ate. The cleaners came and went, and were happy to meet Molly who greeted them at the door. A contractor also showed up, but he looked at me as if I was crazy when I introduced him to what he thought was my cat. He looked over the damage and told me he could get it fixed the next day.

Introducing Molly to the newcomers was the only real distraction from the computer. Finally, when no one had come up with anything, I decided to call Neil to see if he could give us some extra help. I sat on the couch, and Molly curled up next to me as I dialed the number.

"Dude, you're back home," Neil said as he picked up.

"I am," I said, biting back the reminder that I was a woman. Any friend of Neil's was 'dude.' "It's good to be back."

"There's been some chatter running through the system about your deal in South America."

"What kind of chatter?"

"Military shit. I'm just glad you're back home and Taylor was able to keep you in one piece."

"If he hadn't been there, I wouldn't have made it, that's for sure."

"Like, what's going on now? Taylor said you're back on the job."

"I am. We all are," I corrected. "That's actually why I'm calling. We've run into a type of Lost we haven't seen before. I've been running through MyTH files while the others are checking AIR systems. We can't find anything on it."

"What kind of stuff do you know about it?"

"It's tall. Really tall. Easily over seven foot. It has horns—"

"That narrows it down a lot."

"These aren't like minotaur horns though. They go out and curve back. More like what you'd see on a goat. Its skin looks tough, and there were patches of fur or hair all over it."

Neil laughed. "Yeah, like I bet it had one hoof and one foot."

"It's possible it has hooves."

"Dude, your witness was stoned."

"What makes you think that?"

"He like, got stoned, watched the parade and then freaked out. Either that or he was having a bad trip."

"What parade?"

"The Krampus parade. You know, like, for Christmas."

"What is Krampus and what does it have to do with Christmas?"

"Dude, you've got, like, Santa and then you got the anti-Santa."

"You mean he's like Santa but he steals presents instead of leaving them?"

"No, he leaves stuff. I'm not really sure, but I think he leaves, like, bloody bones or something. Or maybe he eats kids. I've never really looked it up. When you're nice, you get Santa. When you're naughty, it's Krampus that comes down your chimney."

"But Santa isn't real," I reminded Neil.

"Dude, neither is Krampus, but people dress up as him this time of year."

"This person wasn't wearing a costume."

"Some of those cosplayers can get, like, really intense with their designs."

"Is it possible that it really exists?"

"Man, if he does, I'd be screwed."

"One time, you said everything is out there."

"Yeah, man, but like, Krampus? I'll dig around, but I don't think you're going to find anything without some really good hallucinogens."

"Thanks, Neil. I appreciate the help."

"Sure thing, partner. I'll send over anything I find."

Frowning, I dislodged Molly and returned to the kitchen. Instead of diving back into the MyTH files, I did an internet search on Krampus.

"Have a lead?" Logan asked.

I pulled up the images and sat back in my chair, staring at a picture of a creature that roughly resembled the person that stood in my kitchen the previous night. "Not one that makes any sense."

"What is it?" Vincent asked.

"The anti-Santa."

Boone laughed and Rider grinned.

"Say again?" Logan asked.

"Krampus," I said. "A person that is half goat and half demon who punishes naughty children at Christmas time."

"We're dealing with Krampus?" Vincent asked, disbelief leaking into his voice.

"There's no way," I said. "The person from last night roughly resembles some of these pictures, but there's no way we're dealing with some sort of mythological Christmas figure."

"It is almost Christmas," Boone said, still grinning. "Did these people do something wrong?"

"Nothing that we've seen so far," Logan said. "They certainly weren't kids, though."

"What made Neil think of an anti-Santa?" Vincent asked.

"He's stoned," I said. "That and there was apparently some sort of parade on TV the other day with people dressed up as Krampus. He's going to keep looking to see if he can find something else."

"As long as he doesn't have us chasing Santa next," Vincent said.

"I'm going to call it a day," I said after checking the time. "I've got dinner plans." Feeling a note of tension at the words, I quickly added, "With Mom, Bob, and Gran. I'm going to get ready. Gran put some leftover stew in the fridge if anyone wants anything."

Upstairs, I quickly went through the physical therapy exercises for my arm, changed my shirt, and then did the best I could with my hair using one hand. When I stepped out of the bathroom, I found Vincent leaning against my desk.

"You look nice," he said.

"Thank you." I could feel my cheeks redden at the compliment. "Sorry I forgot to tell you I had plans."

"You don't— I mean you're not..."

"Not what?"

"There's a lot of things we haven't discussed. About us I mean."

"We haven't discussed anything."

"We should," Vincent said.

"Maybe. You know, we haven't even gone on a date yet, not a real date."

That seemed to surprise him. "You're right."

"What is it that you want to talk about?"

He looked slightly uncomfortable, although I would have bet I was the only person that would notice.

"Downstairs," he said, "I was worried you thought I might be upset because you said you had plans."

I grinned. "I didn't want you to think I was seeing someone else."

"If you were, it's none of my business. Like you said, we haven't even been on a date."

My smile faded fast. "Are you seeing someone else?" I almost added, 'again,' but I managed to hold my tongue.

"No, and I'm not interested. But I don't want you to feel like you're trapped with me."

That's what this was about. I went to Vincent and took his hand. "I've never felt trapped with you."

Our energy reached out and swirled together, blending seamlessly.

"And if this hadn't happened?" Vincent asked. "If I hadn't taken a small piece of your soul? Would you still feel the same?"

"Sharing a soul gave us an advantage in knowing each

other a little better. If we didn't each have a piece of each other—"

Vincent shifted uncomfortably.

I knew he hated the idea that I might have a piece of his soul, so I hurried on. "It might have taken longer to get close. You're not exactly forthcoming with how you're feeling, but if I managed to find out what type of person you are—"

Vincent stiffened and looked stormy. "I'm a killer, Cass. I hurt people. You of all people should remember that."

"It's not like you run around hurting people indiscriminately."

Vincent glared and moved away from me. "I do, though. Why do you think I left in the middle of the night when I stayed? I can't risk it."

I crossed my arms, not wanting to hear what he was saying. "I'm not worried about you being next to me."

His voice grew cold. "I don't have that luxury."

Why did it always have to come back to this? "Do you regularly suck out people's souls when you sleep next to them?"

"I'm smart enough not to find out."

A small part of me felt sorry for him. Always staying away from people sounded lonely. Most of me was tired of this argument. "I've slept next to you before."

"In the woods, when our guards were up and we were sleeping light. This is different."

My heart felt squeezed. "You didn't do anything to me the other night."

"It's been less than a month since I hurt you. It's not going to happen again."

"That wasn't—"

"Don't kid yourself by thinking it wasn't me or wasn't my fault. What happens if I have a nightmare, a real nightmare while I'm asleep next to you? I'm not willing to risk it."

The realization of what that might mean hurt and brought tears to my eyes, but I refused to let them fall. "So, this is the way you want it to be. You forever holding me at arm's length."

He looked wary and didn't say anything. It took me a moment to realize that he knew what I felt. *Maybe he thinks he pushed too far.*

Maybe he had.

Either way, I had to get out. "I'm going to be late," I mumbled, and moved towards the door.

"Wait, Cass—"

"Don't," I said, holding up a finger to stop him where he was. I took a deep breath and tried to calm down a little. "I'm not suggesting that we jump into bed together or start living with each other. If you want to wait, that's fine. You want to go slow, that's no problem, but what you're doing is cutting things off before they even start."

I hurried out, not giving him a chance to reply. Downstairs, I didn't even look towards the kitchen where I assumed the others were still working. I thought about saying bye, but I knew that Logan or Rider had probably heard what happened. *It's possible they decided not to listen, but how likely was that?*

Instead, I grabbed my coat and left without a look back.

One of the worst parts about getting upset with Vincent was that he'd know about it. I couldn't let myself get sad, cry, and then get over it. He'd know exactly how I felt, which didn't seem fair. I could get an idea of how he felt, but only when he was there in front of me.

Was this how he wanted things to be? He said he wasn't interested in seeing anyone else, and I knew he wanted to be with me, but that seemed to mean something different to him than it did to me. He had a purely physical relationship with his last girlfriend—at least that was what he claimed. It didn't seem like that was what he wanted with me, but eventually, I wanted to wake up next to him.

Eventually.

That realization helped. Everything with Vincent was intense, like tonight, but we were once again getting ahead of ourselves. He wanted to keep his distance now, but it was possible that would change later.

It was also possible that he'd never change his mind. Would I be okay with that?

Luckily, I didn't have to figure it all out tonight.

I'd gotten control over myself by the time I met Mom, Gran, and Bob for dinner. Mom was trying hard to keep things upbeat and normal for Bob, and the rest of us kept pace. She didn't even say anything about my arm being in a sling, which I thought for sure would elicit comment.

Gran must have known something was going on. She told me that later in the night, I needed to give someone a chance to explain.

By the time dinner was over, my trouble with Vincent seemed minuscule by comparison to what my mother was going through. She was watching her second husband die. Gran had seen three husbands pass.

What was wrong with me? I was getting worried over what seemed like trivial issues in light of Bob's illness.

I wanted to call Vincent as I walked back to my car. The problem was, I had no idea what to say. Was I sorry? Well, not for what I said—not really anyway. I was sorry we argued. Maybe I could start with that.

Maybe he would still be working at the house. Instead of calling, I could see him.

"Cassie?"

I froze and inwardly groaned.

"I thought that was you," Zander said as I turned to face him.

"It's me."

"I'm glad we bumped into each other."

"Why?" I hadn't meant it to pop out quite that way, but I was glad it did.

"You seem to be doing really well."

My forehead crinkled in confusion.

"Well, something's different anyway," Zander said, his smile growing wide. "An inner glow or something."

What? "Well, thank you. I guess." *How can I make him go away?*

"We should get together sometime and, you know, catch up."

To my great relief, my phone rang.

"I don't think that's the best idea," I said. "Work's calling. I have to take this. Have a good evening."

As I walked away, I glanced at the caller ID before answering. It was Ethan, so it turned out I hadn't even lied to Zander.

"I'll see you around," Zander called.

I didn't turn around or respond. Whatever Zander thought he was doing, I didn't want any part of it.

"Hi, Ethan," I said. "You have the best timing."

"Cassie, I'm glad I reached you." A quiver was in his voice that I hadn't heard before.

"Did something happen?"

"I needed to talk to you. Are you free to come by my house?"

Checking the time, I saw that it wasn't even nine o'clock yet. The day seemed never-ending.

"Sure," I said. "I can stop by."

"Alone," Ethan said quickly. "If you don't mind."

That sounded odd. "Sure." Maybe someone on the team said something to him earlier in the day. "I'm not far away. See you in ten minutes or so."

I hung up and switched gears to the case. Since I wasn't the lead, the only thing I could think he might want was for me to use my powers for something. I started running through excuses to say no before I stopped. It surprised me that I hadn't even considered trying to read something. It had been weeks since I've used my ability, but that was no reason to say no automatically. Besides, that might not even be what he needed.

His living room appeared dark from the outside, but it looked like maybe his kitchen light was on. When I knocked on the door, he hollered, "Come in!" so I let myself in.

Ethan's house was warm and familiar. I hadn't been there often, but I'd enjoyed the time.

"I'm here," Ethan called.

I dropped my coat on a chair and headed towards the light of the kitchen. I smiled at Ethan, who was sitting at the table, but facing the living room. Then I took note of his expression.

My feet were still moving on their own, right towards him. When his eyes darted to something, I followed his gaze.

What came into view looked wrong in the bright light of the kitchen. Horns glistened. The person's rough skin had scars that stood out in stark relief to the fur around them.

I felt myself going for my gun.

Which of course, I wasn't wearing.

"Don't," Ethan said. "It's okay. I think."

"What do you mean, it's okay?" I moved towards Ethan, wanting to put myself between him and the Lost. I wasn't sure what I was going to do when I got there. Without my powers or a gun, and with my arm in a sling, I was useless. The realization that I was at the mercy of the creature in front of me froze me in mid step. My breath seemed to seize in my chest, and I looked for the exits.

The creature didn't move.

My phone rang, and the room filled with a music that sounded sharp and harsh in my terror.

"He's not here to hurt us." He was silent for a few seconds. "I think."

I could have done without that last part.

"He broke into my house last night," I told Ethan, my voice coming out shrill. I turned to the creature, trying to remind myself that it was a person. "You broke into my house!"

His rough face contorted, creases deepened and pushed new scars into relief. "Broke out of your house."

"What?" I snapped.

"I broke nothing on the way in." The voice was gruff and coarse. He all but growled his words.

"Well, you broke everything on the way out!" To Ethan, I added, "He's killed people."

"No," the man said. "I've harmed no one and I will not harm you now."

"You're damned straight you won't," I said, as though I could somehow stop him if he tried anything.

"You must listen," he said. "I am here to ask for your help."

"My help?" I asked.

"Your team. You, the werewolf, the elf, the other humans. I need them. You must take me to them."

"Not a chance."

The creature shifted slightly. "I could ask them to come for you."

It was a subtle yet clear threat.

"Hey," Ethan said, raising his voice. "That's not what we talked about."

"I was making a point. It is not an intention."

"What exactly was it you talked about?" I asked, glaring at Ethan. "What are you doing?"

"I wouldn't have called you here if I thought he'd hurt you. I think you should hear him out."

"You don't look too sure of him," I said, putting as much accusation in my voice as I could.

"I'm sure, just... I'm not used to dealing with something quite like this. I think a golem was the scariest thing I've ever seen until now."

I let out a long slow breath. He was right, of course. Ethan would have no idea how to deal with a monster in his kitchen.

Hell, I didn't have any idea how to deal one.

"We have a witness," I said to the strange person. "The witness saw someone of your description next to the murdered victim."

"Yes, I inspected the body."

"Inspected?"

"Yes. I am tracking the killer."

"Why are you after him?"

His face wrinkled across the forehead, and the mouth turned down. "It is my job."

"You don't work for AIR. We would have known by now if you did."

"I do not work for anyone in this world."

"Why should we believe you?"

"Because I tell the truth."

"If you're legit, then you'll let us take you into the office to check out your story."

He shook his head. "I will not."

"Why not?"

"We need to capture the killer first. Bringing in an organization will slow my hunt and more will die."

I opened my mouth to disagree, but then closed it again. He wasn't wrong. "What's your name?"

"It will make no sense in this language. Your world has referred to my people as Krampus. You may call me that."

If I wasn't still half terrified, I would have laughed. "I'm not calling you Krampus. That's not a myth that someone in your field will want to be associated with. Your supposed field."

He seemed to think. "Someone from your world called some of our people as Billy. Will that work?"

My first thought was Billy Goat, but I didn't want to get hung up on something trivial. "Billy will do. How did you get here?"

"I followed someone who has done great harm in my world, and now in yours."

"I haven't seen anything about a portal opening." Would I have seen something? I was sure Hank would have mentioned once we started on the case.

"I know nothing of how these things are discovered here. We entered yesterday."

"How do you know our language?"

"It is similar to my own. Our people used to travel here often."

"The person you're chasing, why did he come here?"

"Many know the Paths to get to this world. It's not something we allow anymore."

There were a hundred questions that I wanted to ask. Trying to narrow them down was proving to be a challenge. "How do you know the races of the people on my team?"

"After last night, I knew I would need help. It is not easy to travel in your world unseen."

"This killer you say you're chasing, how is he managing it?"

"Much of his ancestry is human. He might look out of place, but not so much that he would draw attention."

"What makes you believe him?" I asked Ethan.

"He's had a chance to hurt either one of us, but he hasn't. His story seems to line up."

The scarred appearance, complete with sharp teeth and goat's feet, made me automatically think the worst. That and the fact that he had broken into my home. Nevertheless, I knew I couldn't make a judgment on a person because I might be afraid of them.

"Entering my house without being invited was a mistake," I said. "I'm not sure I trust what you say."

"I made a mistake at your house last night," Billy said. "I

did not think I would be welcomed if I waited to be allowed entry. When I came in and the creature attacked, I was unsure of what to do. It is a formidable beast for one so small, but I didn't want to risk hurting it, so I escaped."

"Had you hurt her, you wouldn't have made it far." Normally that might have been true, but right now, it was an empty threat.

"What are you keeping in your house?" Ethan asked me.

I stared at the monster straight out of mythology and I knew I needed my partners on this. I also knew that there was no way I was going to trust this thing alone with anyone.

"Her name's Molly, and since I need backup, I'd love to introduce you to her. Mind helping me get our new friend here to my house?"

"We can take my truck," Ethan said.

"Thank you. Okay, Billy, here's the deal. I don't trust you, but you do have a right to explain yourself to the team. What I'd like to do is take you to my house. On the way there, and while we are there, Ethan is going to keep an eye on you. Know that if you do anything, it's not going to go well for you."

"I understand. I should disclose that there is not much a human can do to me to stop me. It's only the elf or werewolf that could do me harm."

I rolled my eyes and shook my head.

Ethan laughed. "That might be the case for a normal human, but—"

"Let him think what he wants," I said, interrupting. "But I know at least a bullet will slow you down. Ethan, do you mind bringing your gun along?"

"You take it," Ethan said. "You'll be more effective if something does go wrong. I'll drive."

We had Billy lie down as best he could in the back of

Ethan's truck. As long as he didn't move around, no one would think too much of about what we actually had back there. I kept myself twisted in my seat the entire ride, watching Billy as he laid still and prone in the back.

While I watched, I called Rider, asking him to meet us at my house. Between him and Logan, Billy could be subdued. I wouldn't have to use my powers and risk hurting him, and Vincent wouldn't feel forced to take him between the dimensions, or worse.

When we stopped at my house, I jumped out of the truck bed. "Don't move."

"I have no intention of harming anyone," Billy said.

"That's good, but stay put anyway. I need to introduce Ethan to Molly. I'm not sure what she'd do if you came in at the same time. If you stand around outside, my neighbors are bound to see you."

Ethan started to look nervous. "If it's better for me to stay outside, I will."

"No way." I passed him his gun and walked to the door, constantly looking behind me. "Besides, I think you'll like Molly. Wait here."

I stepped inside and flipped on the light. Keeping my voice low, as to not wake Boone yet, I called out to Molly. She trotted into the room quickly.

"I've got someone for you to meet." I held up a finger and said, "Be nice."

I opened the door for Ethan and ushered him in. "Just stand still while she gets to know you."

Molly growled and began to prowl around Ethan.

"I didn't realize you'd have company," Vincent said. He had frozen halfway down the stairs. "It was getting late, but I thought I'd wait..."

Tension rode high in the room, and Molly snarled.

"Um, should she be doing that?" Ethan asked.

A part of me had hoped Vincent would be waiting for me, but I hadn't thought about what it might look like to him.

"She's fine," I told Ethan, "as long as you stand still."

Vincent unfroze and continued down the stairs. "I'll take off. We can talk tomorrow." His expression was blank, but even without the Path open I could sense his turmoil.

"No, don't go."

I could see his jaw clench and his eyes harden. "I really think it's better for everyone if I do."

I was torn between waiting near Ethan while Molly did her thing and going to Vincent. Vincent won.

"It's not— Ethan is here for the case," I said.

"Sure." I was probably the only person in the world that could see the skepticism in Vincent's face. "The case."

I tried not to glare at him, but it didn't work. "We can talk about this later. Is Boone here?"

"I think so," Vincent said.

"Good. Go get him and call Logan if you don't mind. Ask him to come over. Rider is already on his way."

"He is?"

I gritted my teeth. "I've already had to deal with Zander tonight. I don't need this." I shouldn't have said it, but it was late, I was tired, and my arm was starting to throb once again.

Ethan seemed to be ignoring Vincent and me, for which I was grateful, but he didn't let this pass by.

"You saw your ex?" Ethan asked.

I gave him a weak smile. "I told you, you had good timing."

"You need to be careful around him."

"He's harmless, just annoying."

Ethan gave Vincent a look, which only made me crankier.

"Molly's done," I said as she jumped onto the back of the

couch and watched Ethan closely. "Can you go get our friend? I think I'll hold Molly when he comes in."

Vincent walked up behind me while I petted Molly and Ethan left the room.

"Sorry," he said. "I didn't mean to make things worse."

"Then maybe trust me a little?" I felt a little guilty for saying it, but I was aggravated and it was the best I could do.

Surprisingly, he smiled, although it looked sad. "It's not you I don't trust. It's me."

"I should have called and warned you," I said, picking Molly up and not looking at him.

"You didn't know I was here."

"No, but I wanted you to be."

He stepped in front of me and scratched Molly behind the ears. She purred and rubbed against his hand.

"You ready for him?" Ethan asked.

I looked at Vincent. "Do you have your gun on you?"

"Yes. Why?"

"It's probably better that you keep it holstered—at least for now. Keep on your guard, but remember, I invited this guy here for a reason. It's okay, Ethan." I walked to the door. "Let him in."

Billy ducked his head under the door and came in.

Molly shrieked.

"It's okay," I said, trying to calm her. I was distracted by Vincent grabbing my arm, trying to pull me back. "Stop, it." I tried to shrug him off. "I'll drop her."

He let go, but moved in front of me, not taking his eyes off Billy. "What's going on?"

"It's just possible that we may be after the wrong bad guy. That's why I wanted the team here."

"You're sure?" Vincent asked.

"No, which is why I want you to stay on your guard. Let me introduce Molly before she hurts herself."

"Give her to me," Vincent said, without looking away from Billy. His eyes were flat black.

"It has to be me or Gran that introduces her."

"Not this time." Vincent took Molly. Her fur had puffed up, making her look almost twice the size she was.

When Vincent stepped forward, Billy stepped back and hit his head on the wall above the door.

Vincent grinned, but not in a nice way. "You know what I am?"

Billy nodded, and said nothing.

"Then you'll know what I do if you make a wrong move."

"I am not here to hurt anyone," Billy said.

"Let's keep it that way," Vincent said. He approached and Billy arched back. Molly growled and started to sniff. She was not a happy ichneu. "Cass, do you mind getting Boone? We'll wait here."

"Play nice," I told him before dashing upstairs to get Boone.

It took a while to rouse Boone, and I called Logan when I knew he was getting dressed and coming down. When I dashed back down the stairs, I found everyone standing where I had left them. Molly wasn't as puffed up as she had been before, but that appeared to be the only change. Even Ethan hadn't moved.

"Are you going to keep him backed up in a corner?" I asked. "I wanted you to hear what he had to say, not bully him all night."

"What the—" Boone didn't finish the sentiment, but the way his gun jumped to his hand was disconcerting.

"Billy, why don't you take a seat?" I suggested, hoping if he were in a less threatening position, my team wouldn't be so antsy.

"How did you find him?" Vincent asked.

"I didn't. He went to Ethan's house and Ethan called me."

For the first time since Vincent had seen Billy, he looked away from him. His eyes narrowing in on Ethan. "You called Cass in alone?"

Ethan looked unnerved and wisely didn't reply.

EIGHT

Eventually, Vincent relented. He put Molly down and let Billy enter further into the room.

Once Rider and Logan arrived, my living room was crowded. Rider stood over Billy like a sentry, but Vincent didn't step far away. I stepped away and got drinks for everyone, while Boone and Logan began the interrogation. Molly sat on the back of the couch and glowered at the newcomer.

When I found out Billy hadn't eaten anything since he'd arrived, I also heated up the rest of Gran's stew for him.

During the questioning, I didn't learn much more than Billy had already told me. It did surprise me that Logan seemed fairly quick to believe the story.

"Do you have any idea where our suspect might be?" Logan asked.

"I have a strong notion about the general area," Billy said. "That's why I needed to reach out to you. If I were to go after him, I would cause a good deal of chaos among the local population. I am more likely to get apprehended than he is."

"You're not wrong," Boone said.

"What happens if we find him?" Logan asked. "What are your orders?"

"Once we have him in custody, I must follow local law first," Billy said. "He's killed here as well. If your agency allows me to take him back, I will. If not, and if he will remain in custody here, I will return to my world without him."

"Where is he hiding out?" Logan asked.

"I don't know the exact location, but I will know when I get closer," Billy said.

"How?" Boone asked.

"He has invoked strong magic," Billy said. "That is how I was able to track him."

"Magic?" I asked.

Logan twisted looking uncomfortable. "The agency we work for doesn't get too involved in magic."

Billy's brow furrowed. "It's my understanding that magic remains hidden in your world, as well as the Lost. You hide and protect the Lost, but do nothing with the magic?"

"Our job deals with other dimensions," Logan said. "Most of our magic users are locals. Anyone that's been around three or more generations is usually off our radar."

"If you are unable to keep him contained in your world, I will have to take him back with me," Billy said.

Logan shifted again. I could see his mind working over-time. "If we catch him, we can take a detour before taking him back to the farm. MyTH may be able to find someone who can bind him."

"Permanently?" Billy asked.

"They'll get us someone who can," Logan said. "We'll take you out tomorrow to narrow down the location."

"And tonight?" Vincent asked.

"Tonight, we get some rest," Logan said.

"I think it will be best if Billy comes to stay at my house," Rider said.

"Are you sure?" Vincent asked.

"I do not think it would be good for him to stay here. My house is out of the way," Rider said. "There is no chance of him being seen."

"It's not a bad idea," Logan said.

"You have any trouble," Vincent said, glancing at Billy as though he wanted to make sure he was listening, "you call me."

"Expect a late start tomorrow," Logan said. "I'll get in touch with MyTH to see if they can help us out."

In what seemed like moments, the living room cleared out. Rider and Billy were off to Rider's house in the country. Ethan and Logan weren't far behind. Boone disappeared back to bed, leaving Vincent and me alone.

He sat down on the couch next to me, and I leaned into him automatically. Being close to him felt as natural as breathing. He sat rigidly for a short while, but then put his arm around me and relaxed. Energy flowed between us, and I basked in the feeling, content.

"I'm sorry for earlier," Vincent said.

"For before dinner or after I came back?"

"Both."

"I'm glad you stuck around. Are you staying the night?"

He tensed.

"Gran said she put new sheets on your bed."

"You don't mind?"

"I think it's a good idea. My arm will be better in a few weeks, though. Maybe then I can tempt you to stay with me again."

He pushed my hair back and kissed my neck. "I look forward to that."

SLEEPING while Vincent was only a few walls away would usually have been a fruitless endeavor, but once again, my medicine dropped me straight to bed.

The morning started without me. The sound of a power saw jolted me out of bed. It took my brain a few minutes to catch up to the fact that there were construction workers in the house and that no power-saw-wielding demon had cut its way in.

Painfully, I stretched my way through the physical therapy exercises and then got ready to face the day.

Downstairs, I waved to Boone in the living room, before looking in at the kitchen. There was a giant hole in my wall, it was cold, and Molly was agitated, watching every move the workmen made.

"Thank you for letting them in," I said when I joined Boone.

"Vincent took care of it. He wanted to make sure Molly didn't try to chew on any of them."

I grinned. "Where is everyone?"

"Out. Billy has them driving around town trying to catch the trail of our killer."

"What are we supposed to be doing?"

"According to Dr. Yelton, you've got an appointment. I'll take you there and then we can meet up with everyone later in the day."

Boone was smart to start with Dr. Yelton's name when telling me about the appointment. Even so, I was cranky about having to drive to the farm for what ended up being a checkup and real physical therapy. The only good news was that my arm could be out of the sling a few hours each day, and in a few days, I might even be able to forgo it completely.

By the time we returned, it was late afternoon. With workmen at the house, I was pretty happy that we only stopped to gear up and go meet the others.

Gearing up might have been an overstatement for me. Boone let me have a flashlight and my gun. I'm pretty sure the only reason he let me have my gun was because he couldn't understand someone getting by without one. At least not while on the job.

It was still light when we parked the car. We walked a few blocks and met the others at the truck. It would have been cramped with all of us and Billy, but apparently Billy was too big to sit up front, so he'd been riding around in the back of the truck all day. Knowing what he thought of Vincent, he probably preferred it.

"What do we have?" I asked when I jumped in the back seat with Rider.

"We're pretty sure he's been staying in that building," Logan said, nodding toward a large building under construction. "Billy tracked the magic back to here. There's a lot of it hanging around."

"It's likely he doesn't risk staying there during the day," Vincent said. "We looked around the site earlier and didn't find anyone out of place."

"There were a few spots that felt as though magic had been performed, but we have no idea what he might be up to."

"This would be his third night in this world, right?" I asked.

"Yes," Billy said, talking through the barred space between him and the cab of the truck. Most of the time we keep it closed, so it startled me when I heard his voice so clearly. "I am not sure he spent both nights here, but the traces we've found indicate that he might have discovered this place the first night."

"What's this guy's name?" Boone asked.

"Darvick," Billy said. "That is a rough pronunciation."

"Looks like the crew is leaving for the day," Logan said.

"Do we have a plan?" I asked.

"Rider and Vincent are going to circle around to the back and enter from there. Ethan is already inside, talking with the contractor. I'll go in and meet him before everyone is gone. We'll wait inside for him to come back. You, Boone, and Billy will wait out here. You can let us know if you see Darvick approach the building."

"And then what?" I asked. I didn't like the idea of sitting outside, twiddling my thumbs.

"We'll let you know if we need you," Logan said. "If he tries to leave, stop him."

It wasn't a bad plan, but that didn't mean I liked it. I didn't do well with sitting back and watching, but with my injuries it was probably the best place for me. Admitting that sucked.

After Vincent passed out the comms, they were off.

"Sorry you're stuck out here with me," I said to Boone.

"I rather think that he is outside because of me," Billy said. "I do not think your partners trust me."

"You broke into my house," I reminded him.

"I broke out."

"You came in without permission," I corrected. "Why did you come to my house anyway?"

"You seemed to be the most approachable."

I rolled my eyes. "Because I'm a woman?"

"I do not know," Billy said. "Even from a distance it feels as though...."

"It feels as though what?" I asked.

"You are friendly," Billy finished. "That is not quite the right feeling, but it as close as I can come up with."

"That's usually the opposite of what people tend to think."

"I don't know," Boone said. "We saw that in the jungle."

"The spiders?" A small shiver ran through me when I pictured the orange spiders the size of basketballs.

"And the snake. Don't forget the monkeys."

"I liked the monkeys." I had almost forgotten about them.

"Even my team thought you were approachable. Not that they trusted..." Boone broke off.

His team was never far from my mind. The last time I used my powers, I died. The time before that, I killed a teammate. Not on purpose, but that only made it worse. Trying to forget about it, to shove it into the back of my mind, hadn't worked well. I still saw Davis every night in my nightmares.

"It's starting to get dark," Boone said, changing the subject.

"We're in place," Vincent said through the comms. "Just inside the back door."

"Ethan and I are positioned near the front door," Logan said. "The last of the crew is on their way out."

I opened my link to the comms. "Are there only two doors?"

"The others are blocked," Ethan said. "No one is getting through them unless they can walk through walls."

I cut off my mic and looked through the bars, trying to see Billy in the darkness. "He can't, can he?"

"What?" Billy asked.

"Walk through walls. You mentioned magic."

"It is not likely. Much is possible with magic, but making an object permeable would take a lot of power. That would be a waste when there is a door."

"Good point," I said.

Now we wait. I didn't say it out loud. There was no need to.

Waiting around for something to happen was one of my least favorite things to do. With memories of our last mission plucked from the recesses of my mind, I knew it wasn't going to be a pleasant, so I tried to take my mind off Boone's former team.

"What's your world like?" I asked Billy.

"There are a few different races living together in my world," Billy said. "The occasional other race will slip through, but they are not hidden the way they are in this world."

"Is that why Darvick can pass as human?" I asked.

"It is. His skin is more scarred and rough like mine, but his build is human."

"Why is your skin so scarred?"

"It is difficult to notice trivial cuts. We heal fast, so the cuts scar. Scars enhance your status in my world. Your skin shows how hard you work and how you live your life."

"Molly seemed to bite pretty hard," I said. "I noticed you don't seem too concerned about it now."

"It will heal soon. Another scar. It is very different here, with smoother skin. Darvick will stand out in a crowd, but he can pass without comment among most humans."

"Speaking of Darvick," Boone cut in, "I think he's on his way." Boone switched on his mic. "We have someone heading straight for the front entrance. Could be our guy."

Leaning forward, I gripped the seat and watched the lone man approach, and then enter the construction site.

Maybe waiting wasn't the worst thing. Having to sit outside while my partners were inside with a murderer was a horrendous feeling.

"Why aren't they saying anything?" I hissed to Boone, not wanting to raise my voice in case I missed something over the comms.

Moments later, gunfire rang out. Once. Twice. Followed by a cold silence as the wind picked up.

"Come on," Boone said.

Despite my arm, I was out of the truck almost as fast as he was.

Billy strode up quickly from behind as we ran down the block towards the construction site. "Magic is being used."

"Someone is going to see you," I hissed to the rough-looking creature.

He looked around guiltily, but continued with us.

The tingling feeling I had expected to feel didn't come. For some reason, I thought I'd be able to sense magic, but apparently, I didn't have the knack.

Boone stopped around the corner from the main entrance and turned his comms back on. "Update?"

My breath froze in my chest as I strained to hear any hint of a reply. The lack of response was somehow deepened by the howl of the cold air that began to whip down the street.

"Get ready," Boone said. "We're going in."

I took off my sling and dropped it. The wind soon dragged it down the street. My gun was already in hand and my heart thudded hard.

Boone silently slipped around the corner and quietly padded down the street. He moved quickly, confident that I had his back and he didn't have to worry about what might be coming up behind him.

Unfortunately, the click of Billy's hooves on the sidewalk broke the quiet. Surely, with the wind, though, that wouldn't be noticed inside. Right?

There was no way to look into the building. Glass door and windows probably wouldn't have lasted long during this stage of construction. We'd be going in blind.

We readied ourselves, and when Boone quietly pushed open the door, we swept inside, guns at the ready.

The main floor was nearly skeletal, but a few walls were up, blocking the view of the others. We saw nothing. My bad arm curled around me as dull pain began to take hold. When we heard voices, I forced it back up, ready to steady my gun when needed.

When Boone nodded, I followed him around the corner, both of us training our guns on a scarred man that stood in the middle of the room.

"More guests," Darvick cackled. "Aren't I the lucky one?"

"Put your hands up," Boone said, circling around the man.

Ethan and Logan stood nearby Darvick. Logan was on the balls of his feet, practically bouncing. His face looked stretched and angular. It was a wonder that Ethan stood so close to the elf. When he elfed out, Logan exuded an intense aura of fear and aggression. Ethan stood only a few feet away, something even I would have been hard pressed to do. Granted, he didn't look happy about standing so close.

Why weren't they attacking?

"Stop moving!" Logan yelled at us.

Out of the corner of my eye, I saw Vincent and Rider. My mind screamed out to keep Darvick in sight, even though all I wanted to do was check over Vincent and Rider to ensure they were unharmed. It helped that Logan had told us to stand still. If he said it, there was sure to be a reason.

"It's no matter," Darvick said. He flicked his hand towards Boone, making odd motions in the air, and then uttered a few words I couldn't make out.

"Stop!" I yelled. "Put your hands up."

"Shoot him!" Logan called.

I hesitated. It was so unlike Logan to say such a thing, especially when it was obvious he wanted a fight, but magic was in use. That had to be what Darvick was doing. Who knew what that could lead to?

I shot once, aiming for his lower half. Darvick growled, distracted by what I had done, but I must have missed. As his hand drew up to wave in my direction, I fired two more times.

Billy roared and charged into the room just as Darvick gestured towards me. Something hard hit me in the chest, bowling me over backward, and tossing me into the metal framing of a wall. When I hit the ground, my breath was sucked away. I struggled desperately to fill my lungs until one breath shuddered into me. Gasping, I rolled over and tried to take in the situation once again.

Billy was close. Very close. But it seemed like he was beating against air between himself and Darvick, unable to move forward.

Darvick didn't look happy now. Despite the cold, sweat glistened on his face.

"You bastard!" Darvick spat at Billy. "This isn't even your world!"

Tentatively, while Darvick ranted at Billy, I tried to aim at Darvick once again. However, as I brought my hands up, I hit something and could move my hands no farther.

CHAPTER

NINE

A wall of air. It was a trick I had used myself several times, bringing together a solid wall in the Path. I pressed against my cage and rose to my feet.

Magic.

Shakily, I found the edges of my prison, hoping it was only a wall. It was a hastily put together irregular shape and only a few feet wide. If I fired my gun, there was a good chance it would ricochet, coming back at me or stop as the wall caught it.

"You can't hold these circles forever," Billy growled.

"Forever isn't needed," Darvick said. He seemed to have reined in his anger, at least for now. "One or two sacrifices here and I'll be on my way. I've always wanted to know what elf blood would do to my magic." He began to walk wide around Billy, toward Logan. "Walker blood would surely taint everything, but another human would do. And I have so many to choose from."

Darvick moved towards Logan and Ethan's invisible cell.

Logan bounced, his ears at their points, and his hands looked like they were itching to grab the man.

Logan could end this. I knew he could. With his elfin strength and fighting skill, he could take out Darvick the moment the cage fell away.

It was as though Darvick read the intent. "I'll keep you alive. The spell demands that the blood be taken from a live person. But that doesn't mean you will be conscious. A short time without air should do the trick." He grinned at Logan and put his hand up to what looked like empty air.

Within moments, Logan was returning to his human form. Both he and Ethan looked like they were breathing hard.

He was going to kill them. Darvick was going to kill my partners.

I looked wildly at the others. Boone pounded against his cage. Rider followed suit and pushed. Vincent looked much like Darvick. Vincent's eyes were closed, and it seemed as though his hand was pushing against empty air. Billy ran his hands over the cage.

What the hell was Vincent doing? What could I do?

Entering the Path was my only option, but it hadn't worked for weeks.

It was my only option. Knowing I had to work fast, I put my best efforts into it right away. I didn't waste time with half-assed attempts to force myself into the Path. Instead, I sat cross-legged on the floor and tried to push away the world around me. I breathed deeply a few times to calm myself. It didn't take long to realize that calm was out of reach. Less panicky would have to do.

My mind stretched to the dark abyss that stood between the Path and me. Ignoring the smooth shards of my soul, I jumped.

Nothing happened.

I tried again.

Still nothing.

If I could reach Vincent, the extra burst might be enough to push me through, but there was no way to make that happen. Or, if Vincent could get free, he could suck out Darvick's energy, which might do the trick, but again, that seemed impossible.

Logan was feet away, dying, and I could do nothing. Tears started rolling down my face, and I began to try brute force to reach the Path.

Even without reading the Path, the air was thick with panic and anger. Sensing that, stirred an idea. I opened my eyes and watched Vincent for a moment. He was trying to pull energy from the cage. That had to be it.

Shifting directions, I closed my eyes again and started to try to sense the magic in the room. Since I had no idea what I was looking for, it took me a few moments to realize I had found it.

Moments that Logan and Ethan didn't have.

It was energy of a sort, and I knew the Path was there, even if I couldn't see it. Hoping I was concentrating on the magic of Logan's cage, I pulled.

There was a slight shudder to the cage. I could feel it.

As soon as I stopped pulling, the prison walls snapped back into place.

Glancing up, I saw that Darvick looked worried. In their cage, Logan wasn't moving, but Ethan looked as though he was breathing a little easier.

Pulling the energy would work, but I had to put it somewhere. Thoughts of fighting a demon flashed through my mind, and I knew what would work.

Logan was out, but hopefully, I had bought him a little

time. I tried for Vincent's cage. Instead of concentrating on moving the energy, I dragged it into myself.

Fizzy, popping sensations slowly began to fill me. I heard Darvick say something, but I didn't pay attention.

Under my breath, I spoke to Rider. "Tell Vincent to get ready."

When the cage broke, the remaining power rushed to me. I opened my eyes to see the results.

Darvick stood over me.

He kicked me hard. My body involuntarily curled up from the sharp blow. I felt oddly relieved that he hit me on my side. It could have been worse.

Darvick bent over me and grabbed my shirt. A roar from behind him filled the room, and he let go.

With Darvick distracted, I pushed myself away from him and got back to work. Ethan and Logan came next. It was easier the second time. The magic felt jittery in the room, as though it was quivering and wanted to break free. As it entered me, I began to feel like I was floating.

Boone was next. I started to feel giddy when his prison fell.

Wanting to see the fun around me, I opened my eyes. Darvick was on the ground. Boone dragged Logan away.

With my mind bubbling with magic, the noise of the room started to bother me, so I started to hum to block out the sound. This is what we were good at. The thought of our team made me smile.

Vincent had a death grip on Darvick, but Rider tried to pry the hand away. It was clear that Darvick wasn't getting back up.

Vincent batted Rider away with his free hand and I giggled. Vincent turned my way and let go. The room blurred, but Billy was still locked away. Enjoying the cold concrete floor, I laid down and began to work on Billy's cage.

"Cass, whatever you're doing, stop," Vincent called.

I grinned and kept humming. The last of the magic snapped away, and my mind swam.

I rolled over on my back and stared at the ceiling. My muddled mind decided it was a good ceiling for staring at. Billy approached and I smiled broadly at him, but Rider called him back to look over Darvick.

Soon my best friend was crouched down over me, looking me over.

"My friend," I mused. "My fine, furry friend."

Rider frowned and looked around to see if anyone else was close by.

"Oops," I said. "My bad."

"Can you stand?" he asked.

I thought about that. My body felt as though it were riding waves, so I decided standing might not be the best idea.

"Let's try for sitting," I suggested. "Is everyone okay?"

"Everyone but Darvick. Vincent should know if he will wake up, but I have not asked."

As Rider pulled me up, the world stood still and moved at the same time, leaving streaks hanging in the air. I tried to touch one, but apparently couldn't reach.

"You have many new bruises and other damage, but nothing that should cause odd personality changes," Rider asked, probing my head. "I do not know what is wrong with you."

"Everything is awesome." I giggled and started to lay back again, but Rider stopped me. I let my head loll back instead.

"It's the magic," Billy said, one hoof on Darvick as though the unconscious man may move.

"What about the magic?" Vincent asked, pulling Ethan to his feet.

"She has it," Billy said. "All of it."

Vincent's eyes widened slightly, but I was willing to bet I was the only one who noticed.

"That can't be good," Vincent said. He glanced at Logan, who was sitting down against a wall.

Logan shrugged.

"Can you let go of it?" Vincent asked.

"Why?" I asked.

"He killed people making that magic," Vincent said. He looked back and forth from Billy to Logan and back again. "That has to taint things, doesn't it? What's that going to do to her?"

"Apparently, it's going to get her high," Logan said.

"Bingo," I said, and laughed again.

"Magic is not inherently good or evil," Billy said, looking thoughtful. "But this was created using the blood of others. I'm not sure what that means for the energy itself. When will Darvick wake up?"

Vincent shrugged noncommittally.

"Could be a few days," Logan said.

Vincent frowned at Logan before turning to me. "Try letting it go, Cass."

I sighed and closed my eyes again. The magic I had taken from Billy's cage was still at the forefront. It was trial and error to actually release the power. Being addled by its strength didn't make it easy.

Finally, it burst forth. Rider was flung aside as it passed. It was as though the werewolf weighed nothing.

By the time I sucked in a breath to yell out for my friend, it was over. Rider rebounded and jumped back to his feet, looking shocked but unharmed. I felt heavier, as though more grounded than I had previously been.

Billy left Darvick and moved to where he had been captured. He pushed against the hardened air, and then he walked around it with his hand out following the unseen surface.

When he stopped, he dropped his arm and looked at me. It wasn't exactly a friendly look. "I know you did not recast the spell and a spell can't recast itself. What was done here?"

Logan stood and joined him, although unsteadily. "I don't think she got rid of the spell. She only stripped it of it's magic."

"The magic is the spell," Billy insisted.

"Perhaps not," Logan said.

"It's not the way things work," Billy said, his voice rising.

"Can we argue about this later?" Vincent snapped. "There could be side effects we aren't seeing. She needs to let the power go. You can fight over what it is or isn't later."

"What will happen when the workers return tomorrow?" Rider asked. "It will be hard to explain why they cannot go into certain areas."

"It will disperse on its own," Billy said. There was a touch of a growl in his voice.

"That might not be the biggest issue," Logan said. "There's no sign of spellcasting here. Somewhere, there's evidence floating around, and I'd bet it's in this building. Otherwise, he wouldn't have bothered with the traps."

"Traps?" I asked.

"Magic traps," Logan said. "That's what those things were. We triggered them. He added yours at the last minute. We can get Hank to call in another team to check the place over. For now, we should leave the room. Who knows what path the magic will take once she lets go of it."

Billy glared at me. For some reason, this struck me as incredibly funny, and I didn't bother trying to contain my amusement. Billy rolled his shoulders before returning to Darvick and heaved him over his shoulder.

Vincent came over to me as the rest left the room.

"Get her back to the truck when you can," Logan said. "Let us know if you need help."

Vincent nodded.

"Ready to let this go?" he asked after the others had gone.

"Not really," I admitted. "I feel all bubbly and light."

I sensed an uncertainty coming from him.

"Do you want to keep the magic?" he asked.

"*Yes.*" I smiled up at him. "But the question is, should I? I'm thinking it's not the best idea."

He relaxed and sat down beside me, putting his arm around me. "I agree."

I leaned into him and wished my coat wasn't as thick. "I think you should move behind me. Just in case."

He didn't move away while I was close to him. When I sat up, he placed himself behind me and put a hand on my shoulder.

The fizziness of the magic had blurred together somewhat. When I closed my eyes, I concentrated on teasing out the magic of a single spell, but the melding made it impossible. Instead, I mustered my strength and pushed it all away at once. It exploded out of me, and the magic snapped back into place.

It felt as though lead weights fell on me. What was worse, pain, new and old, came back in full force. I groaned and laid back, but Vincent stopped me.

"What's wrong?" Vincent asked, trying to keep his face impassive.

"Why did that asshole have to kick me?"

Vincent moved back around in front of me and started to unzip my coat.

"I'm fine," I said, grabbing his hand. "I just need a minute."

He froze as though unsure of what to do.

"Anything broken?" he asked when I didn't add anything.

"Just bruised."

"And the magic? It's gone?"

"It seems to be." I didn't add that it was worse than a hangover now that it was gone. However, that probably had something to do with being tossed around and kicked, so I kept my mouth shut.

"Where's your sling?"

"I couldn't use my gun as well, so I tossed it off. It's long gone."

Vincent allowed himself a sigh.

I decided a change of subject would probably be in order. "Are you sure Logan's alright?"

"Yeah, Boone checked him over."

"And Ethan?"

"He was better off than Logan. I checked him out, but he's not even bruised and never lost consciousness."

"I wonder if elves need more air than humans."

"Best not to speculate. At least not while on the job."

"You're right about that."

"Think you can manage standing?"

I made a face, but nodded. Vincent offered his hand and pulled me up.

The pain in my injuries shifted in intensity, some worse and others better while standing. The feeling of being weighed down didn't get any better, but it wasn't any worse either.

"I'm so ready to go home," I said. "Let's get out of here."

CHAPTER

TEN

"You lost the sling," Paulson said, moving down a chair so that I could sit.

"Thankfully," I said, trying to pick out my partners in the crowd. The bar was practically crawling with federal agents. There were three at our table that I didn't even remember seeing before. "I don't think I've ever seen so many coworkers in one place outside of the office."

"There was that raid in Eugene and the one at that abandoned farm."

The conversations around us picked back up and the noise level rose significantly. "I was thinking away from work. Getting together like this isn't a regular event."

"Well, it's not often coworkers show up at the office weeks after they've been assumed dead. It's worth celebrating."

"It was a good idea. Everyone looks like they could use the break."

"Did your team pull the holiday shift?" Paulson asked.

"I think it'll be quite a while before we get a break."

Paulson leaned back in his seat. "That doesn't make sense

to me. It's obvious you all had a hard time. Most people would get a few weeks of comp time."

"It's complicated," I said

He grinned. "It usually is."

The best I could do with that was smile.

"Logan seems to be bringing in the festive cheer," Paulson said, nodding toward my partner at the bar.

Sure enough, the elf wore a Santa hat and he was telling a story that seemed to be fascinating people.

Paulson's focus shifted behind me. I didn't have to turn around to realize Vincent had arrived. Had the situation not been so distracting, I probably would have noticed as soon as he walked in.

"It's good to see you here," Paulson said, getting up. "Have a seat. I'll get us drinks."

Vincent took Paulson's place. Our table grew noticeably quieter, and I could sense a rising tension. Several men shifted in their seats, but Vincent looked unfazed.

I tried to ignore the change in atmosphere and smiled. "I wasn't sure if I'd see you here."

"Paulson talked me into it," Vincent said. "Have you seen Rider?"

"Not yet, but he texted and said he was on his way. I've been meaning to ask you. Do you want to come over for Christmas this weekend?"

A slight raising of his eyebrows told me I caught him off guard.

"I mean, if you don't have other plans. I wasn't sure if you visit your sister or other family. But if you're around, you're welcome to join us. Logan's family comes over, and Rider will be there."

By the time I finished rambling, he was practically smiling.

"If your family is okay with it—"

"Mom practically insisted," I said.

"I brought a pitcher," Paulson said, setting down a few glasses before taking a seat next to Vincent. "Where are Boone and Rider? I thought they'd be here by now."

"Rider's on his way," I said.

Vincent looked at me, and I could see his eyes pinch together in concern. "Boone's not going to make it."

"I thought he was coming," I said. "We just talked this morning."

"He went into the office and got held up." Vincent looked uncomfortable.

A feeling of wrongness sprung up. "How? We don't have a case."

"A military delegation arrived this afternoon." Vincent glanced at Paulson quickly before looking back at me.

"Yeah," Paulson added. "I saw them come in. Hank wasn't too happy with them showing up the way they did."

My eyes grew wide, and I looked around for Logan, half expecting to see military men arriving.

Vincent put a hand on my leg. "We don't know what they want yet."

The tingle of the connection helped rein back my sudden panic, but the words weren't helpful. "If Boone is held up, we know exactly what it's about, though."

"It could be a formality," Vincent said.

"Yeah, right," I said. "A formality could be taken care of through a video conference.

"Is Boone in some sort of trouble?" Paulson asked.

"We all are," I muttered.

"It's too early to say," Vincent said, trying to cut me off.

"Did your last mission go that badly?" Paulson asked, lowering his voice.

"We didn't do anything wrong," Vincent said, "but there's some people that probably wished we had stayed dead."

I didn't let myself look at Paulson or Vincent. "You mean you didn't do anything wrong." I tried to keep everything that happened buried, but Davis crawled out of my mind while I slept and reminded me. It seemed to be eating away my abilities. Maybe if I told the truth—

"Boone would be dead if you hadn't done anything." Vincent glanced around to see if anyone else was listening. It seemed that only Paulson was paying attention. "We all know that."

A part of my brain tried to tell me that was true, but most of it told me I was kidding myself. If I had intentionally used my powers to stop Davis and Tolman, it would be a different story.

Vincent looked uncertain. "Let's go talk—"

"It's fine." I tried to shake the thoughts out of my head. Wrong time, wrong place. I plastered a smile on my face. "We're back, and that's what tonight's about. What are we drinking?"

Paulson looked concerned, but rallied. "They have a local brew on tap. I thought we'd give it a try."

"Sounds good," I said, trying a sip. It wasn't bad for beer. "Did you meet Billy?"

"We've chatted a bit," Paulson said, relaxing some. "There's no way I'd pass up a chance to talk with a Krampus. It's too bad we couldn't get him here."

Billy had been stomping around the office, waiting for his prisoner to wake up. "I tried, but he didn't like the idea of being in public."

"I don't think AIR would be too keen on the idea of letting him come to a bar," Paulson said.

"Good point," I said, grinning. "Excuse me for a minute. I'll be right back."

I hurried to the restroom, which was blissfully empty. My outward mood turned to match my inner mood, and I paced the floor in front of the mirrors. The idea of leaving Boone alone with anyone from the military was horrible. My stomach tried to twist, so I took a few deep breaths.

We knew this was coming. Boone knew what he was doing.

If I went in, it would only make things worse.

Especially if they tried to keep me.

Not that I personally could do much right now, which was a huge problem. I'd gotten lucky on our last case. To expect to get by without reading again would be asking for trouble.

That's what I should be doing now. Fixing myself in order to be ready for what comes next. Whatever that might be.

Having a direction cheered me up considerably. I was still worried about Boone, but I could do my part and I would.

The smile came a little easier this time. When I stepped out of the bathroom and spotted Rider leaning against the wall, waiting for me, the smile even became real.

"Vincent wanted me to check on you," Rider said. "He appeared very worried."

"Vincent always worries. You are just the person I wanted to see," I said, hooking my arm around his.

"I am?"

"You are. Are you free tomorrow?"

"I will be helping Margaret in the afternoon. Is she really starting to cook tomorrow for dinner this weekend?"

I laughed. "She is. She and Mom are determined for this to be the best Christmas ever."

"My morning is still free."

"Excellent. I need to start meditating again. Do you mind helping me out again?"

"I thought Vincent would want to help you."

"I'm not sure he'll be the best meditation partner for me. I'm sure he can help, but things get... complicated with Vincent and me together."

"That is true. I will be happy to help. I've missed meditating together."

"Me too."

We arrived at the table and I took my seat next to Vincent.

"I will be busy the week after Christmas," Rider said, taking an empty seat across the table.

"What's going on that week?" I asked.

"I will be taking a vacation."

"Vacation?" Vincent asked. It was clearly the first time he was hearing about it.

"Yes."

When Rider didn't continue, I prodded. "I didn't realize you were taking off work."

"Angel called today," Rider said. "She will be free. I have never taken time away from work, so I thought I would try."

"Who's Angel?" Vincent asked. I was pretty sure even Paulson could read the surprise on his face.

"She works for MyTH," Rider said.

"That's great," I said before Vincent could break in with a string of questions. "I'll muddle through with Vincent that week."

"Muddle through?" Vincent asked, raising an eyebrow.

"That does sound like an accurate description," Rider said. He looked like he was trying not to smile and failing miserably at it.

"I thought so." I was almost as good as Rider at keeping a straight face.

Want to read further?
Eclipsed Pathways (AIR Series Book 10)

WRITING the AIR series has been a fun and amazing experience. There's more planned for Cassie and her partners!

IF YOU ENJOYED THIS BOOK, please leave a review on the site where you made the purchase. Leaving a review helps the reader and author in many ways. Your support is appreciated!

THANK YOU FOR READING!
Amanda Booloodian

COMPLETE WORKS

Complete works by Amanda Booloodian:

AIR Series (In Reading Order)
Stonecoat: Novella 0 (AIR Series Book 0)
Shattered Soul (AIR Series Book 1)
Redcap (AIR Series Book 2)
Broken Paths (AIR Series Book 3)
Stolen Sight (AIR Series Book 4)
Fenrisúlfr: Novella 3.5 (AIR Series 5)
Fractured Worlds (AIR Series Book 6)
Reliquary (AIR Series Book 7)
Never-Ending Nightmare (AIR Series Book 8)
Krampus (AIR Series Book 9)
Eclipsed Pathways (AIR Series Book 10)
Void (AIR Series Book 11)
Marked Soul (AIR Series Book 12)

AIR Series Box Set

AIR Series Books 0-4: Welcome to the Farm
AIR Series Books 5-8: Conspiracy Theory
AIR Series Books 9-12: Redacted

Spellbound Murder Series

Oath Bound (Spellbound Murder Series Book 1)
Grim Magic (Spellbound Murder Series Book 2)
Fallen Witch (Spellbound Murder Book 3)

Spellbound Murder Box Set

Spellbound Murder Complete Trilogy

AIR Series Audiobooks

Stonecoat: Novella 0.5 (AIR Series Book 0)
Shattered Soul (AIR Series Book 1)
Redcap (AIR Series Book 2)
Broken Paths (AIR Series Book 3)
Stolen Sight (AIR Series Book 4)
Fenrisúlfr: Novella 3.5 (AIR Series 5)
Fractured Worlds (AIR Series Book 6)
Reliquary (AIR Series Book 7)
Never-Ending Nightmare (AIR Series Book 8)
Krampus (AIR Series Book 9)
Eclipsed Pathways (AIR Series Book 10)
Void (AIR Series Book 11)
Marked Soul (AIR Series Book 12)

Spellbound Murder Series Audiobooks

Oath Bound (Spellbound Murder Series Book 1)
Grim Magic (Spellbound Murder Series Book 2)
Fallen Witch (Spellbound Murder Book 3)

ABOUT THE AUTHOR

Amanda Booloodian lives in Missouri with her loving, and often times peculiar, husband. She has been passionate about the written word throughout her life. Now, much of her spare time is spent at the computer, delving into worlds accessible only through vivid imagination. In warm weather, when she isn't pounding on the keyboard, she can often be found wandering through the wilderness. Occasionally she gets it into her head to SCUBA dive or to sit back at home and make wine, which can have interesting results and inspire her writing.

You can find out more about Amanda and her writing, including upcoming releases, on www.Booloodian.com. You can also find her on Facebook: Amanda Booloodian - Author and Instagram: AJBooloodian.